W9-ATT-337

My need for freedom, for my own life, was stronger than anything. *It had to be.* It had to be. This time, one way or another, I would shake him. For good and for all. I was going to have *my* life, not Denny's life. But how?

A SMALL WHITE SCAR

K. A. NUZUM

JOANNA COTLER BOOKS
HarperTrophy®
An Imprint of HarperCollins*Publishers*

Wholehearted thanks to

Dr. Lee Krauth

M. T. Anderson

Marion Dane Bauer

Alison McGhee

Holly McGhee

Justin Chanda

Joanna Cotler

Karen Nagel

A Small White Scar
 For information address HarperCollins Children's Books, a division of HarperCollins Publishers, 10 East 53rd Street, New York, NY 10022. www.harpercollinschildrens.com

Library of Congress Cataloging-in-Publication Data

Nuzum, K. A.

A small white scar / by K. A. Nuzum.— 1st ed.

p. cm.

Summary: Fifteen-year-old Will Bennon has always looked after his twin brother, Denny, who has Down syndrome, but now Will is ready to leave his family's ranch and become a professional cowboy, but Denny unexpectedly joins the journey.

ISBN 978-0-06-075641-3 (pbk.)

[1. People with Down syndrome—Fiction. 2. Brothers—Fiction. 3. Twins—Fiction. 4. Cowboys—Fiction.] I. Title.

PZ7.N967Sm 2006 2005017721

[Fic]—dc22

Typography by Larissa Lawrynenko ❖ First Harper Trophy edition, 2008

This book was made possible, in part, by a grant from the Society of Children's Book Writers and Illustrators.

09 10 11 12 13 CG/CW 10 9 8 7 6 5

To Willard, the cowboy of my heart,
and to Brent, my first friend in the world.

A SMALL WHITE SCAR

1

IT WAS CLOSE TO MIDNIGHT. The crickets sang loud and steady. The July air was so hot and heavy it made me sweat just to push each breath from my lungs. From my cot on the ranch house's screened front porch I picked out the single stars and constellations in the black Colorado sky that Momma had taught me when I was little.

The Northern Cross stretched its arms wide across the Milky Way. All the dimmer stars were washed out by the light of the round, white moon, but in the south, Vega still shone bright.

A coyote keened and wailed close by. I held my breath and strained my ears, trying to tell if it was the devil I'd been gunning for the last months. The one that chewed up my dog Lucille so bad I had to shoot her. I'd spotted him at least a dozen times, him and his stubby, damaged tail. I'd even fired a couple shots at him, but I was never close enough. Though he was always far distant, I felt like I knew him. I'd seen him hunt and knew he favored ground squirrels for dinner, but didn't care for their tails. He always gnawed them off and left them stiff and dry on the ground. His paws were narrow but thick-padded; his prints jumped out at me from all the other coyote tracks that crisscrossed the ranch. And I knew he was a loner; his tracks showed him always solitary, never with a pack, never with a companion. I was the only one in the wide world, I figured, who kept track of him, cared where he was and what he was up to.

The coyote's prickly voice joined with Denny's snoring across the porch; and I felt like I'd jump out of my skin.

Denny always snored. Most nights I had to get up and roll him over on his cot to make him stop. I never slept through the night.

I folded my arms behind my head and bent them so they covered my ears. I had figured up that if Denny had been snoring for fifteen years, snoring every night since 1925 when we were born, that meant I'd been tossing and turning for over five thousand nights.

No, sir, I never slept through the night. But it wasn't always Denny's snoring that woke me first; sometimes it was the dream.

That night I got in a good two hours of sleep before the dream woke me up. In the dream, it was me and Denny out riding. When we reined in we were far out on the prairie. It was late in the day, and the weather had settled in so I couldn't even see the mesa. No rock outcroppings. No junipers, no piñon pine. There was only Denny and me. I turned to remind him to keep the reins loose when he jumped down so he wouldn't tug on Scooty's mouth. His arms were too short, so he always ended up yanking on the reins when he got off, and that made Scooty back up, and then Denny would get his foot stuck in the stirrup and have to hop backward to keep up with her. Half the time he ended up on the ground, scraped and bruised and feeling disgusted with himself.

But when I turned, Denny was already down and waiting on me. And he was changed. His face wasn't all slack anymore, his eyes weren't small and slanted, and when I looked into them, I saw that he looked just like me, instead of like a cartoon drawing of me.

Finally, I thought, *my real twin brother*. This was how it was supposed to be. I was so happy.

I felt like a five-hundred-pound boulder had been lifted off my shoulders. This was what I'd always wanted.

I would keep looking into Denny's eyes and begin to see myself reflected there. I had changed too. *My* face was all lax, *my* eyes were tilted up. I had a big ol' grin spread ear to ear.

And that is when I woke up every time. And every time, my heart pounded in my chest, my breath so fast my head spun, and my cheeks burned from the hot tears running over them.

I pulled on my jeans and boots and eased the creaky screen door open. I stepped into the night and took a deep breath that filled me with relief.

I was alone.

Denny was asleep. He would not follow me.

My father was asleep upstairs and wouldn't tell me to go check on Denny.

Deep heard me. From over in the corral he gave a nicker. I pushed through the hot air to the rail fence.

His light, ghostly form moved toward me, and as it drew closer, took on his regular, beautiful horse shape. He nudged his soft, whiskery muzzle into my hand and blew. The other horses wandered over too, thinking I might have food. They all ambled off again pretty quick. Except for Deep.

Deep and I were partners, *compañeros*. We were about as close as a two-legged fifteen-year-old and a four-legged eight-year-old could be. We depended on each other. We liked the same things, too: speed, competition and freedom.

Deep's name was no accident. He was the deepest-bottomed horse there ever was; he had the endurance of three horses. He could outrun any in a short race and outlast any on a long haul. He was a quarter horse, a roan with a mane as black as pitch and a tail the same, except for a tuft of short hair at the base, which was stark, stark white. His flanks were the lightest gray with black and brown spots, like an Appie, but smaller. The spots didn't show up until he was almost three, then everybody tried to get me to change his name to Dice, but it was too late. He'd already shown the stuff he was made of, and he was Deep.

A longing built inside me. Deep pawed the ground. "Okay," I said. "I can't sleep anyhow; there's too much to think about."

I reached into my pocket and gripped the roll of bills. I had saved for a long, long time, and I had twenty-five dollars for my entry fees. In just a few days' time I would compete in my first professional rodeo. A tingle of excitement zipped through me; I could almost hear the master of ceremonies' voice crackle over the loud-speaker: "Welcome, ladies and gentlemen. Welcome to the La Junta Rodeo of nineteen hundred and forty."

I would win the purse in all my events. I would claim the big prize money as the Overall Winner, and I would show all the hands there that I had the best cowboying skills around. Every ranch represented at La Junta would want to hire me, and I would sign on with one of the out-fits. I would work for six weeks on the new spread, and then I would go north to Cheyenne for the big rodeo.

Our foreman Hank said when he competed up there in 1930, he won two years' ranch wages in just two bull-dogging events, and bulldogging was never a good payer. There was no real danger in steer wrestling—no real skill either, just a few tricks—so it never drew many entrants, and since most of any purse came from entry fees, bulldogging wasn't worth much. You also had to give the hazer, the cowboy who helped run down the steer, a cut of the cash.

Calf roping always filled up. Good roping called for skill and practice, so the winnings were always high. If twenty ropers entered at La Junta, I figured the purse could go over two hundred dollars, and that was close to half a year's earnings for a top hand on a big ranch. I'd spent years working on my roping skills; my toss was more accurate than anyone else's on my father's ranch, or on any neighboring spread. I could hardly wait for fresh competition.

Riding rough stock paid the best, though. The only thing more dangerous than a bucking horse was a bucking bull. Either way, by hooves or horns, a cowboy's career could be cut short, and that's why the money was always good. Next to roping, riding bulls was my best event.

I would send part of my winnings home to help with expenses on the ranch and to help smooth things over. My father would storm and rage when he found I had left school and everything else for good and all. But I would be sixteen at the end of the summer, the same age he was when he struck out on his own. It was my decision.

I went to the wooden shed and felt along the wall for the nail that held Deep's halter. He followed me, and as soon as he saw what was in my hand, he lowered his head. I slid the halter up over his nose and tied a D knot in it at his cheek. I brought the loose end of the lead rope around in a circle and tied it to the other side of the halter under his chin, and then slipped the circle up over his ears and neck for reins. I bent low and pushed off hard so I landed with my lower belly across Deep's back. I swung my leg over, straightened up, and picked up the rope.

The other horses gathered around as we made our way to the gate, but I opened it just wide enough for Deep and me and then swung it closed behind us.

The silhouette of a hootie owl flapped silently over our heads, lit in the top of a piñon and called. An answer came from down by Calf Pasture Reservoir. I turned Deep toward the sound, and we eased into the darkness. A warm breeze puffed up from nowhere and lifted my hair, dried the sweat on the back of my neck.

2

I RODE DEEP RIGHT UP the middle of the reservoir. I could see that a few head of cattle had crossed the basin a couple weeks before, when the loam was still soft and moist. The scorching sun had since baked the shallow edges rock hard and uneven with the cattle's hoofprints. The bottom was so dry it had cracked into a million stepping-stones. The water was gone with the drought. All that remained was a small puddle at the west end with moonlight floating in it: Momma couldn't have drowned in this.

Even Denny wouldn't have blinked at the thimbleful of water. It wouldn't have made him start to yell the way a full bathtub did. The minute he heard the water running in the tub, he started to grunt, and then he bawled, and then he screamed.

Just the way he had seven years before when Momma slipped and cracked her head on the rocks at Pacheco's Water Hole and we watched her disappear into that deep, black water.

I slid off Deep and squatted down. Deep nosed the puddle, but didn't drink. With water in the corral trough every night, he wasn't thirsty all the time like the range cattle were.

A cloud slid in front of the moon, but even without its light, I knew there were more than cattle hoofprints around the tiny pool. All the wild creatures were feeling the drought. The mule deer, coyotes, black bear, mountain lion; they all used our reservoirs.

Rain had been falling all around us. Ranchers to the north and west said they were catching regular storms, but they didn't have extra grazing land to lease, so we moved our cattle from dry pasture to dry pasture, trying not to overgraze any area too badly, while we watched black storm clouds heavy with rain track away from the ranch.

More and more ring muhly, with its silver-green blades curled into stunted nest-shapes, was coming up in the pastures and gaining a hold where good grazing grass like blue grama had been thick just two years before.

I ran my hand through the muddy, tepid water at my feet; my shoulders tightened. I was leaving behind a pretty serious situation. If the drought didn't break, some of the cattle would die, money would be lost, precious land might have to be sold.

But my leaving wouldn't change any of that. It wouldn't leave Father shorthanded; it wouldn't leave him with no one to talk decisions over with. He'd just have to find a new nursemaid for Denny. I shook the muddy water off my hands and swung back up on Deep. We turned and rode north toward home.

3

"IT'S NOT RIGHT," I shouted, and I grabbed my hat off my head and threw it to the ground at my father's feet.

Last night I'd felt sure of myself after my ride with Deep. I'd had my plan and my future waiting for me to ride into it in two days' time. But now, with morning's light, my father had ambushed me and was trying to steal that future from me.

"Look," he said. "I know you practiced real hard to get ready for La Junta. But that rodeo goes on every year. You'll have another chance at it, but if I leave those cattle here even a few days more, they'll starve. This is our livelihood, boy. I got good pasture leased for two hundred head, and I'm going to move them."

My temper was running fast, and I knew if I didn't settle myself, I wouldn't stand a chance. Father thought the only things to show feelings about were low beef prices and drought.

"I worked this whole year for it," I said, calm and steady. "And it's only seventy miles. I leave day after tomorrow; it's only five days—two days there, one for the rodeo, and two home—I'll be back Monday. You could go first thing Tuesday morning."

I didn't look at my father because that was not the truth. I would not be back on Tuesday. I would not be back.

He shook his head.

"Nope. Drought's got too bad, boy. Showing off in a rodeo isn't worth losing stock for."

"I'm not showing off, I'm—" I stopped myself just in time. "You don't need me here. You've got a perfectly good foreman to run things. You give him final say over my opinions anyway."

"*Will.*"

"Sir."

I scuffed the sole of my boot back and forth in the dirt next to my hat. Bits of gravel bounced off it.

"It's not the ranch. You know that." He said it low and tight.

"Hank can look out for Denny, too. If he can look after the ranch, he can look after Denny."

I glanced up. Beyond my father I saw Denny creep past the corner of the barn. He didn't like rows; he was going to watch the ants out in back of the ranch house to calm himself down.

My father's harsh silence drew my eyes back to his face. It was red, swelled considerably. A lot of the normal creases in his skin were smoothed out from the pressure that was building inside of him. My mother used to tell him he'd die of the apoplexy from holding things in, but she died instead, and he just got quieter and redder.

"God durn it, boy!" He yelled it through clenched teeth, so the noise mostly stayed inside him. "He's your brother. The same blood runs through his veins as runs through yours."

He paused, his mouth set, and then locked his eyes onto mine so I couldn't move.

"I'm counting on you. Look after Denny." My father stood quiet for a minute and then turned and walked off quick, his shoulders hunched. The back of his neck was red too.

4

A QUARTER OF AN HOUR later my hackles were just starting to lie down when my father's hard voice cracked the air.

"Hank!"

I saw Hank's shoulders tighten as he handed me the wrench and straightened up from the base of the windmill, turning toward his boss.

My father strode across the road to stand between us.

"Put Jose on that broke windmill, and you get down Cobert Canyon and bring that bunch of cattle up. I want them in the herd going with us tomorrow."

My father didn't look at me; I didn't look at him.

"They been down there days longer than they should; won't be anything but thistle coming up there next year."

"I'll do it," I said. "I'll move them up right now.

There's only fourteen or fifteen head."

I started jogging away from my father, hoping.

But my father had had too much practice. He started his sentence by stopping me.

"Denny. Where's Denny, Will? Go get him started collecting the chicken eggs. Hank'll tend to the beeves."

I looked at Hank. He shrugged his shoulders. Hank had taught me bronc riding and bulldogging, not standing up to my father. He didn't know how to either.

I did not remind my father that the reason he knew that pasture was overgrazed was because I rode down there myself and told him. I just turned around and headed for the anthills behind the ranch house.

Denny would be lying on his stomach in the dirt watching the ants come and go. Lying there waiting for me to tell him what to do next. He would be lying there like he was four years old instead of fifteen. It didn't matter if my father was off on a weeklong cattle drive or if he was on the ranch; it was my job to see that Denny ate, and Denny washed, and Denny didn't walk off a cliff. I always had to be his nursemaid instead of doing a man's work on the ranch.

* * *

Denny was lying in front of the largest mound, his legs spread and straight out behind him. His arms were tucked under his body so his hands cushioned his hips, which always pained him because they popped in and out of the sockets so often. His head was turned away from me. His cheek was planted on the ground so he could see the ants real close.

He should have remembered it was time to collect the eggs. It was his job, not mine. I should've been working alongside the other men.

Denny was so intent on the ants, he had no idea I was behind him. I could give him a bad scare . . . but it wouldn't change anything. I still wouldn't get to herd the cattle; I'd still have to remind Denny about the eggs.

I walked up quietly; I couldn't help myself. When I was right next to his feet I yelled "Denny!" as loud and hard as I could. His lumpy body bounced off the ground, his legs bent at the knee so his boots waggled in the air, and he let out his scared animal grunt.

I felt a deep, mean guffaw work its way up my throat until Denny rolled over. His slanty eyes, the same blue as mine, were open real big, and his cheek, scraped across the ground when I hollered, was raw and starting to seep blood. There was no satisfaction. There never was. There was only a sagging feeling in my heart.

Denny sat up gasping and stretched his hands wide on each side of his face. It was our old sign for "scared." He always went back to the signs when he was too surprised, or too scared, too anything. "You scared me, brother Will."

I squatted down beside him and brushed the bits of gravel off his skinned cheek.

"Sorry, Denny."

"All right. It's okay, brother Will."

He made a cross with his index fingers and smiled at me. That was our most private, important sign when we were younger, before Denny could say many words. It meant we were brothers no matter what, that we'd always be loyal to each other.

Both of our left index fingers bore a small, white scar. Denny's ran long ways, mine horizontal. They were both made by our father's penknife when we were six years old and forbidden ever to touch it.

The knife usually disappeared into the front pocket of my father's jeans when he finished dressing, but the morning we cut ourselves, the knife lay forgotten and beautiful on the vanity in my parents' room. Its handle was silver, inlaid with mother-of-pearl, and it held the bright, sharp blade that dug out splinters but also whittled tiny, perfect horses from scraps of old fence posts. It was irresistible.

Right off, Denny nicked his finger pulling the blade out. He crow-hopped in place and whimpered, and then started to yell for Momma.

I grabbed his shoulders and shook him.

"Denny," I said. "We'll both get a licking if Momma hears you. Your backside will hurt worse than your finger."

He kept on bawling.

In desperation, real quick and real light, I stroked the blade across my own index finger so a line of red appeared, and I held it up before his eyes.

"See, Denny? Mine too."

It did the trick; he was so surprised he quit crying, and his jaw dropped.

"How?"

That was Denny's only question word back then.

I shrugged.

"Because we're brothers. Twin brothers, Denny. We

have the same hurt, so we take care of each other. It's our *secret* hurt. Here." I pressed my cut finger against his. "The same blood runs through both of us. Like Daddy says."

Now I felt my shoulders tense up; I pushed his arms down to his sides just like I used to when I was teaching him to talk more than use signs. When I was trying to help him get on better in the world.

"It's time to collect the eggs, Denny. Go get the eggs."

I finished cinching Deep's saddle and turned back toward the chicken coop.

Denny shuffled toward the henhouse door, the blue-painted egg basket swinging from his arm.

For the next three-quarters of an hour Denny would count and recount the eggs. Each time he added one to the basket, he counted. And each time he didn't find one under a hen, he counted.

Those forty-five precious minutes were the only ones in a day I could claim for my own, but if I stuck to my plan, if I disobeyed my father's direct command, I'd have all the minutes of all the days for my own. I'd have my life.

I lifted my shoulders and dropped them, trying to relax. I swung up onto Deep's back and set out on the trail that threaded through two of the eastern pastures on its way down to Cobert Canyon. I figured on giving Hank a hand rounding up strays; that would clear my head so I could think straight about my future.

I'd lived my whole life, so far, in quick bursts of driving cattle and roping calves, a man for a few minutes, a nursemaid for hours. And my father never noticed those few minutes. He never noticed they had added up and made me a better hand than anyone who worked on the ranch for pay, never noticed they'd added up and made me a man.

From Deep's back I unlatched the first pasture gate, shoving it open wide enough for us to pass through. As I closed it, my eye caught fresh coyote scat on a rock next to the gatepost.

I jumped to the ground for a closer look. The coyote had made a meal of small, shriveled chokecherries, grasshoppers, and a ground squirrel. A flash of hope lit down my spine when I spotted the short tufts of tan fur at the spoor's tapered ends.

My eyes searched for more clues. A half dozen

narrow scratches in the dry earth radiating out from the scat showed he was trying to spread his scent to let everybody know they were in his territory. And just moving off the tips of the claw marks, barely visible in the gray dust, was a single print. Left front foot, narrow but thickly padded.

I swung up on Deep again, my heart racing, and swept my gaze along the coyote's trail. He had moved off to the south; for quite a little ways the tall turkey foot grass was bent down along the southern fence line.

Suddenly, my plan, my future, didn't matter. There was only a deep hunger, a hot desire burning through my arms and legs. I wanted that devil coyote. There weren't many hurts in my life that I had power to change or settle, not Denny's feeblemindedness, not Momma's death. But I could do something about the coyote. I could give him back what he'd given my dog and my heart. I could kill him dead.

I turned Deep, following the coyote's trail and let my eyes roam out ahead.

Just starting up a rise, disappearing behind the shelter of a rock, I caught the wave of a scrawny, tan flag. My stomach jumped; I'd know that tail anywhere, only a third as long as it was supposed to be. Probably somebody had chewed on his tail like he'd chewed on Lucille.

I pressed my heels hard to Deep's sides and slid my rifle from its holster. Hank could handle the strays himself, just like my father wanted.

"Hyah! Go, Deep."

Deep's ears swiveled toward me, and he dug his hooves into the dry ground and pounded up the rise.

Ahead of us, the coyote's ears pricked up too; and in the same moment he turned his head to look at us, he broke into a run up the slope.

I kept my eyes stuck to him as he zigzagged behind rocks and slunk behind woolly sagebrush, and I urged Deep on, faster.

I laughed outright when the coyote dodged behind a clump of sage that sat surrounded only by low, flat rocks.

I had him.

I reined Deep up short and raised the rifle to my shoulder.

"I got you, devil." The words hit so hard against my throat, I almost choked on them. I trained the gun's iron sites just above the feathery top of the sage and waited, my heart thudded against my ribs.

Deep shifted his weight impatiently from one back leg to the other.

I drew in a deep breath, real slow, to keep my aim steady.

As soon as that coyote poked his nose above the clump of sage, I'd blast him right between the eyes. I could wait as long as he could.

A tan triangle twitched above the soft, green bush, and I lifted my rifle a fraction more. I was ready.

Deep's ears flicked backward. The coyote's head popped up; he looked right at me.

I squeezed the trigger, firing the shot, and as I did, I heard rocks being kicked and turned over and dry twigs snapping off the scrub oak behind us and Denny's bleating voice.

"Oh, Wi-ill. Brother Wi-ill."

The coyote gave a wave of his stubby tail and disappeared behind a juniper farther up the hill. My whole self collapsed. My shoulders slumped, and my arms dropped the rifle down to my lap. Inside, my stomach felt like it fell so far it would end up in one of my boots.

I turned Deep. I looked down at Denny. His small mouth was stretched wide, grinning with its pointed teeth, like one of the jack-o'-lanterns people in town set in their windows at Halloween. That was the expression he always got when he saw me.

Anger, branding iron-hot anger, flared inside me.

"Denny!"

His mouth unstretched; his little, pointed teeth disappeared; his lips rolled under; and his blue eyes jumped wide.

"You did that on purpose," I hissed through clenched teeth. "Didn't you?"

Denny's eyes dropped to his boots. He drilled one toe into the ground.

"You meant to scare him off before I could kill him."

Denny's face reddened. He started to cry.

"That coyote did not want to be dead." The words sobbed out of him.

"It's the coyote that tore up Lucille, Denny." I made my voice low; I kept it hard. I locked my eyes onto his and didn't let go. "Not just any coyote, the one that almost bit clean through her back leg. The one that ripped her belly open, Denny. *That* coyote."

Denny let out a whimper and a gasp and choked on his saliva. His head bobbed. "I know, brother Will. I knowed which one that coyote was. I saw that tail. But my brain only could think: fur."

I shook my head. "*Fur*, Denny? What are you talking about?"

"His fur that would be red. And warm and sticky. If you shot him dead. And when his eyes didn't close anymore. Ever."

My breath drained out of me in a long, hot sigh. My anger went with it. Everything went with it.

I watched Denny as he sat down on the rocky incline. He gave a little moan as he stretched his legs out before him; his hips would be aching from the long walk.

I raised my eyes to the horizon, across seventy miles to La Junta. My throat was tight. I felt sucked dry, just like the land.

"Okay, Denny. Okay," I said. "Give me your hand, you can ride back with me."

Denny lumbered to his feet and stuck up one short, fat arm. His knuckles were scraped like usual, from not watching where his feet were going and falling down all the time. I moved my left leg forward of the saddle so he could use the stirrup. With him grunting and Deep standing with all four of his legs braced so he wouldn't tip over, I hauled Denny up behind the saddle.

"Remember, hold on to the cantle."

"I'll hold on, brother Will. I will always hold on."

I urged Deep into a trot and then a lope, and Denny clung tight. So tight.

We were almost home before I realized I was finally drawing free breath again. Between Denny's loud gasps and snorts a chant had filled my head, filled my chest like a heartbeat, in perfect time with the dusty rhythm of Deep's hooves. A smile came to my lips, and silently I mouthed the words, made them mine: *I am leaving, I am leaving, I am leaving.*

5

MOONLIGHT STILL DUSTED the top of the mesa as Deep and I climbed onto the flat. As his weight came over each back leg, I felt the saddlebags and my bedroll shift slightly on his rump. I took a long, slow breath of the last of the night air and reined in, turning Deep so we faced the ranch one last time. It was pitch-black. My father had left only the day before with three hands and two hundred fifty head of cattle, and already Milton the cook was taking advantage and sleeping late. Hank would have him up shortly, though. And that meant Denny would get up too. He'd wonder where I was, but he wouldn't think of the words to say right off. After a while, maybe after breakfast, he'd all of a sudden go up to Hank and ask, "Where is Will? Where is brother Will?"

I gripped the reins tighter and swung Deep away from home. My knees were weak as I pressed them against his sides. He burst into a fast lope across the top of the mesa, but Denny's words and then my father's chased us.

"Son, look after your brother."

That was always the last thing my father said to me, as it had been at dawn the day before when he shook my hand and set out on the cattle drive. I had been dragging those words around like a leg trap ever since my mother's death seven long years ago. "Look after your brother" started out meaning different things to me and my father. When he said it, he meant keep Denny out of his hair so he didn't have to worry with him.

I thought "look after your brother" meant help him grow up, help him be a person. I thought that till I was nine. Until Denny and I were nine, and we decided it was time for him to learn to read. I spent days and days going over my old primer with him, getting him to where he could point to every word under every picture as he said it.

"'The tree is green.' 'The wagon is red.' 'The flower is lellow.'"

When he'd done it perfectly six times in a row, we decided to show off to our father.

Denny raced through every page, all the way through the picture of the blue house.

Then he paused. His mouth dropped open, his eyebrows jumped high on his forehead. His eyes, full up with just one question, lifted to our father.

Our father nodded.

"That's real fine, Denny."

Denny's face lit up like a brush fire.

My father reached out and flipped back several pages in the book. "Read me this page again, why don't you." Denny beamed at my father's interest. He stared at the picture of a small, black dog sitting up and begging.

He looked down at the words.

His lips pursed.

My heart pounded.

Denny pointed to the first word. "This."

Pointed to the second. "Is."

I dropped my head.

"A black puppy dog." His index finger jabbed at the words.

Our father stepped closer to Denny and skimmed

his fingers beneath each word. "'The dog is black.' That's what it says, son. What you did was memorize the book, the order of the pages."

All the light had gone out of Denny's face and he shuffled off, and our father lit into me about how I was damaging Denny by setting his hopes too high.

"Feebleminded," he said. "He'll never read. Don't try to make him something he can't be. Take care of your brother. Look after him."

It took me a while to figure it out, but by the time I was twelve or so, I knew the only way I could ever escape the trap of those words was to chew my leg off just like a coyote would in order to free himself. That is what I had done.

Soon we were five miles distant from the ranch, and Deep's hooves ate up another two mighty quick. In four more the edge of the mesa was coming up fast, and while I knew every inch of the mesa's top, and felt fine riding Deep at a dead run over it on the darkest night, its slopes were treacherous and ever-changing. I slowed Deep to a walk, and we started down the far side of the Mesa de Maya.

The last star had quietly left the sky; a new day was

showing up all pink and gold in the east. Maybe, just maybe, everything would turn out. My belly was grinding; I was starving. I reached back to one of the saddlebags and pulled out a fistful of jerky.

Getting food in my belly made me feel steadier, and I let more thoughts slide into my head a little bit at a time.

I was headed into the future.

I had decided I would have a future.

I was leaving my childhood behind and Denny's childhood behind, and I was going to claim my place in the world. Nursemaid no more. Ranch hand, professional cowboy. And lucky were those I chose to work for.

Come the fall, after I had finished rodeoing for the season, I would sign on with another ranch, much to the boss's pleasure, and I would stay clear through branding time to help out, sending money home all along, and then Deep and me would pick up and follow the rodeo circuit for the whole next season.

Maybe after a year, maybe after two, I would compete in the Trinidad Rodeo and go for a visit home. I would only go back when I was sure I had been gone long enough that they couldn't make me stay. Once I was sure my father and Denny knew I was gone for good and all.

I never figured I'd use my cowboying anywhere but home; I never wanted to. Before Momma died my father spent time working with me, teaching me calf roping and everything else I would have to know to contribute on the ranch.

My father would take time during the day to go out with me to the milk pen. He'd work the gate and chase the calves out one at a time so I could rope them.

Sometimes Momma and Denny would come out and sit on the rail fence to watch. I liked it when they did; it made me try even harder. They'd clap and hoot when the calf dashed through the gate toward me.

I'd climb up on Billy, our best old cutting horse, my feet dangling a few inches above the stirrups and my rope spinning like crazy, ready to make my toss.

Once I started getting good, though, the calves weren't so keen to leave the pen. When Father would finally get a calf chased through the gate, it'd just stop dead with its legs spread and locked, staring around, breathing heavy.

And when its eyes lit on me, it was a race to see

whether the calf made it back to the gate first or I got my rope thrown.

"You boys are going to worry those calves to death," Momma would say, and shake her head, but she laughed just the same. Laughing made her blue eyes dance.

I pulled up on the reins and squinted out over the flat prairie. My eye caught a movement out where everything was supposed to look just flat and brown. Slowly, my eyes defined the shape and the colors of a pronghorn antelope.

The older ranchers had tales about big droves of them back in the twenties before they got hunted down. And folks talked of scattered herds of pronghorns grazing and running around from Trinidad to the ranch and from home to the Oklahoma border.

But in all my exploring and riding and roaming around, I had only seen a few.

Now, unexpectedly, a couple hundred feet below me and Deep, and another half mile out to the east, was an antelope I could stare at to my heart's content. The plain lay before us drying brown in the long summer heat, and the lone pronghorn, all buff and white, blended in perfectly. He had probably spotted us, too.

I wanted a much closer look and gently urged Deep to move a little quicker down the hill. I wasn't sure how close we'd be able to get without spooking him. I kept my eyes nailed to him, though, and as we got onto the flat I began to see more of his fine details. The buff color lay across his back like a quilt that had been cut up the sides, revealing the white creature beneath. It draped itself over his white throat in three thick bands, and a chin strap of deep brown seemed to hold the horns on top of his head. The horns were dark too, rising from his forehead just above the large eyes. The first prong looked to start about six inches from the base and the curved tips stood at about ten or eleven inches.

My eyes kept wandering back to his legs, thick and heavy at the hips, but then narrowing down quickly into thin sticks. Horses' legs looked so delicate, so fragile, but powerful, too, designed for running. The pronghorn's legs didn't look like running legs at all. In fact, they looked like they'd snap off in a stiff wind. Everyone always said how fast antelope are, but I sure couldn't tell it by looking. I figured Deep wouldn't have any problem taking the lead over one and keeping it.

A smile crept onto my face as that thought stuck in my head. I reached for the leather strap that held my rope on my saddle and untied it.

This cowboy was going to do a little early-morning roping.

"Hyah! Go, Deep!"

And we were off. I bent low over Deep's neck; the wind hit me in the eyes and made them sting, but I didn't blink. My gaze hung on the pronghorn. I kept my mouth closed tight; I hated it when a June bug hit me in the teeth. Once I accidentally swallowed one. It was scratchy and bitter.

Deep's feet pounded the dry ground, and like always, it felt brand-new, like it was the first time I'd ever flown over the earth on Deep's back. My muscles were tight with excitement; I was electrified by the crazy speed that his thousand pounds of raw power created.

The plain, as we raced over it, wasn't nearly so flat or brown as it looked when we were above it. Yellow sunflower heads beat the tops of my boots as we ran past them and left dark sprinklings of pollen in the creases of the leather.

Six-foot junipers with green arms sprung in all directions made a fine course for barrel racing, and Deep and I weaved in and out between them.

Hank was the one that got me started barrel racing. He couldn't stand to see anything go to waste, whether it was beans in the bottom of a pot or a sinkful of dishwater that had been used only once. I guess he felt the same way watching me mope around after Momma died. All my father's spare minutes dried up after she passed, so Hank started training me. As I grew, bronc riding and bulldogging took the place of the barrels. But Deep and me were still experts.

I leaned into Deep, trying to keep my body soft yet alert, bending and cornering with him. My father always used to say riding a horse is just like dancing if you do it right. I had been to two dances in town; riding a horse was more natural.

I gave Deep the slightest lead to the right. My left leg came forward, closing off his left side, my right leg bent back to open the way for him. My upper body moved the same way, my left shoulder slightly forward, the right one back, and very little, very little pressure on his mouth from the reins.

He responded perfectly, and I went with him, and the music of his hooves pounding the hard, dried earth and my breath, short and quick, filled my ears.

We fast cut our distance to the antelope, and the pronghorn lifted his head and turned toward us. He was still, watching us, chewing, and he didn't seem at all disturbed to see a mean cowboy and a flying horse bearing down on him.

I squeezed Deep's sides with my knees.

"Go, Deep, go!"

Even though he was full out already, he'd be good for another quarter mile at that speed and a fraction beyond it before he started to slow up. He could still keep going at a mighty respectable pace the rest of the day.

The buck still stood grazing, waiting. I had my rope ready. I could feel Deep pulling forward, reading my mind, ready to do his job. Suddenly, the buck's head swiveled away from us, his ears strained forward, he stared into the distance, the muscles in his haunches tightened and he lit out like a shooting star.

I was mesmerized for a moment, my eyes stuck to him as he sprang away. His four feet gathered in a bunch and touched down as one—lightly, so very lightly—but they propelled him up and out, and then he was already another eighth of a mile distant.

I cursed and came down to a lope. I turned my eyes away from the pronghorn to try to see what startled him when Deep and me couldn't. There was a small bay horse and rider coming at full tilt around the point of the mesa. The rider's elbows stuck out to the sides like a great blue heron's knees. A good foot of daylight showed between the saddle and the rider's hind end as the horse thumped toward us.

6

"NO," I WHISPERED. "OH, NO."

Denny. It was Denny. He'd tracked me down. I was cornered. Cold panic swept through me. I stared for a second longer, watched Denny grow larger as he rode closer, and then I tore my eyes away, cut Deep in a 180-degree turn and dug my heels hard into his sides.

"Go, Deep!" I pressed flat over his neck so the wind would not slow us down. We could outrun Scooty; we could escape. The hard pounding Denny's hips would take trying to keep up would make him turn back before long; the pain would be too bad. It would be too bad.

Suddenly, a metallic clank sounded on the ground

below us, and Deep's right rear hoof set down heavier than the others.

My heart dropped. He had thrown a shoe. I was caught; if I kept running, I'd make my horse lame.

I brought Deep down slowly. I slid off him and realized when my feet touched the ground that my legs were shaking. I picked up Deep's right rear foot; the shoe was gone.

The sound of pounding hooves made my eardrums vibrate. I felt Deep turn his head to look. Behind me a boot hit the ground, and four hooves shuffled away from me. Another boot thumped down. My ears prickled as they were bombarded with gasping and sniffing. I was still bent over, holding Deep's back foot. I did not want to look up.

"Hi. Hi, brother Will. What are you doing? Huh?"

"Trying to guess how much this foot weighs," I snapped.

Denny was silent for a moment. "I think you throwed a shoe. I think Deep lost a shoe, brother Will."

I shoved my fury down deep and made my voice steady.

"Well, then help me find it."

We began backtracking, kicking through the dirt and grass. The smell of sage drew me, comforting me and making me breathe deep and long to capture its scent.

Then suddenly, I wasn't smelling sage anymore. I was smelling rattlesnake. I stopped with one foot in the air and grabbed Denny's arm at the same time to make him stop too.

I knew we were within three feet of one, since I couldn't smell them any further away than that. I figured it was a good sign I didn't hear the rattles.

I grabbed up every square inch of dirt with my eyes and found the rattler about a foot and a half ahead and just a little bit to the right of our path. I backed up slowly and pulled Denny with me. I kept my eyes trained to the snake. It was a prairie rattlesnake, outside its usual territory. I had only ever seen one other, brought in by Hank. This one was a granddaddy of a rattler. Close to six feet long, and thick. Thicker than the calf of my leg. It was a sick greenish-yellow color; black splotches started on its head and ran down its sides and back to the end of the tail. Its pupils were tiny slits in the bright sunlight, vertical like all poisonous snakes and dangerous-looking.

There it was, filling up my nose with its musky smell and lying right next to my horseshoe. Stretched out full-length, and not looking like moving was a priority or even a consideration.

"I don't have another shoe with me."

"Boy! I never sawed a rattler that fat. It's a rattler, isn't it, Will? I never sawed one that fat. Look. Look at his rattles."

He had a string of them, all right, and they were big. The ones at the end of his tail were as wide as my thumbnail; the smallest were the size of corn kernels. I counted fifteen sets and whistled.

"What will you do, brother Will?"

"I could nudge him with my rifle and try to get him moving, I guess. I'd do it if it was a massasauga, but these prairie rattlers rile easier; his striking distance is probably as long as I am tall." I shrugged. "Guess I'll shoot him."

I studied the snake again. He wasn't going anywhere.

"You back up some more, Denny," I said. "I'll go get my rifle."

When I returned, Denny was standing another ten

feet from the snake, bent over, his hands planted on his knees. He was nodding at the snake like he was urging it to get going.

Denny turned toward me, watching as I lifted my rifle. "Brother Will, I can move the snake. I can get that snake to go, so you won't have to shoot him."

"Too dangerous."

"But, brother Will, it makes my stomach hurt to shoot him."

I sighed and lowered my gun.

Denny hated killing. When we were little and my father would shoot a steer in the corral and drag him out in the open to butcher, Denny would lope in circles screaming and crying and shaking his hands.

When Momma heard him bellowing, she'd come running and whisk him up into her arms and make a beeline for the anthills at the back of the house.

I asked her once how she came up with the idea of the ants for Denny.

"By keeping my eyes open," is what she said. "Everything you need to make you feel happy is right here on our land—either over your head, under your feet, or in between."

Momma would lie down in the dirt before the anthills and pull Denny down next to her. Long after he quit screaming, long after he stopped sniffling, she would stay beside him, watching the ants.

Denny hated killing.

I shook my head. I was making the wrong decision.

"Okay. But if you get bit, don't say I didn't warn you."

Denny nodded, his face serious. "Okay. That's a promise, brother Will."

"Well, find something to poke at him with, and I'll be ready to shoot, just in case." I pivoted, searching the ground around us. "There. Grab that dead cholla branch over there."

Denny stumbled over to the long piece of dried gray cholla and picked it up.

"Stand as far back as you can."

He shuffled backward, and I lifted my rifle and cocked it. I sited on the snake.

Denny nudged the stick under the snake's belly, and suddenly, the rattler was in motion. Like wind moving through dry grass, it swung left and right, into the S-curve striking position. Its front third moved up into the air and then drew back, its triangle head raised toward Denny.

I was frozen still for a moment, watching the supple movement.

The rattles lifted and vibrated, breaking the spell. I held my breath, and as the snake struck, I aimed at its head and fired.

7

A HISS CAME FROM the snake, but not from its mouth. I heard a splat, and Denny and I looked down at his boots. Snake blood was squirted across the toes of both.

The rattler lay twisted on its side so its creamy belly was up; my .22 had made a hole right through the widest part of its head.

"Thank you, brother Will. You had to shoot him."

Denny's eyes were filled with tears.

I nodded.

"You had to shoot him."

Denny looked down at the snake again and then squatted next to it.

"Sorry, snake," he said.

He looked up at me.

"I feel sad to see his belly up, brother Will. That is not comfortable for snakes."

Before I understood what he was doing, before I could stop him, Denny reached his hand out toward the snake. His hand brushed across the rattler's mouth. The mouth opened and the fangs sank into Denny's left hand between his thumb and index finger.

Denny hollered and shook his arms in front of him, kind of running around inside his own body and not really going anywhere.

"Oh, my God."

I dropped my gun and grabbed him around his barrel chest, pinning his arms down and holding him until he quit jumping. The more he moved around, the quicker the venom would spread through his body.

"It bit me! It bit me, brother Will."

Denny was slobbering all over me cause he was too scared to think about swallowing; he could only cry and shake.

"I know, I know. Hold still now, and let me look at your hand."

"How did it bite me?"

"Shut up for a minute, and let me look."

He was shaking so hard it took both my hands to hold his hand steady. There were little flat teeth marks between his thumb and finger, but the skin wasn't broken. On each side of them were fang marks. One scratched over the surface and didn't penetrate, the other punctured the skin. A fat drop of blood sat on top of the wound, and more was smudged across Denny's knuckles.

"Well," I said, trying to steady my own voice, "he got you, but not very deep."

"But how did it bite me?" Denny's words came out in a groan. "When it is dead, brother Will? I saw that it is dead."

Denny was nodding, and his eyes were locked onto mine, begging me to agree the snake was dead.

"It's dead, Denny. Now sit down and stay still, I'll get my knife."

I ran the few steps to Deep's side and rifled through my saddlebag. I kept talking to Denny, hoping it would make him calm, and me.

"The snake is dead, but it can bite till it gets stiff. Remember the story Hank told about the one that snapped even with its head cut off?"

Denny whimpered, and bending forward, he threw up on the ground. I gagged and reached back into the saddlebag, pulled out my extra shirt. It was the fancy one with the blue stitching around the pockets and the mother-of-pearl snaps down the front. I was going to wear it in the rodeo. I jogged back to Denny and handed it to him.

"Wipe your mouth." I wondered if he was sick from fear or sick from venom.

How long had it been? I looked at his hand to see if it had started to swell, and then I took my good rodeo shirt from Denny and twirled it into a narrow roll. I tied it tight at his wrist to keep the blood from circulating the venom all through him.

I gripped his snakebit hand real hard with my left and clutched my skinning knife in my right.

"Denny, I have to cut you. I have to make an 'X' right there on top of the bite."

Denny looked up at me, his cheeks sucked in, his eyebrows raised high. "Is it for being brothers? Will you cut your hand too?"

I shook my head.

"No. It's so I can suck the snake venom out before it

gets way inside you and makes you sick. But you have to hold still. Completely still. Okay, Denny? Can you hold still the whole time?"

Denny stared at me; he was working out if that was something he could do. "Okay, brother Will. I can hold still."

I did not wait. I clenched his hand and the knife a little tighter and cut diagonally over the fang mark. A narrow stripe of red appeared. Denny drew his breath in sharp, but he did not move. I cut the other line across the first and dropped my knife and started to suck and spit, suck and spit. I had no idea how long to keep it up, so when my cheeks started to cramp, I quit and rocked back on my boot heels.

Denny used the palm of his other hand to wipe sweat from his forehead. "Brother Will, I want to go home now. Please take me home now."

"Home?"

Every muscle in my body seized up. I felt like I was tied to a post so I couldn't move at all, with a rope around my chest so tight I could hardly breathe. *I can't go home.* If I went home, I would die. My body would still get up every morning and do chores. I would eat and drink and lie awake hearing Denny snore in the night, but I would be dead on the inside. I couldn't go home. I *wouldn't* go home.

I raised my head and looked at Denny. A smear of vomit trailed across his cheek. He held his snakebit hand at the wrist with his other hand, face white as a sheet, eyes wide and panicked. He was making short little jerks with his head in the direction of the horses.

What was I going to do with him? We were miles from home. If there was venom in him, he'd be dead by the time we got there. And anyway, what would they do there that I hadn't already done? Nothing. It didn't make a lick of sense to go back to the ranch. It didn't make sense.

"Denny," I said as gentle and slow as I knew how, hoping he would understand the first time, "you don't want to move around at all for now. You need to hunker down, and we will have to wait and see if that hand is going to swell. If you ride home now, it could make that snakebite worse."

Denny shook his head; he was going to get stubborn.

"I want to go home, brother Will, even if the bite gets worse."

I would have to scare him some more.

"Denny."

I kept my voice low so he wouldn't think I was yelling at him and get all distracted. "You can't go home right now. You could die if you try. This is serious; it's real serious. The only thing that may save you is for you to sit down and breathe deep and wait."

When I saw his body sag, I knew he was going to stay put. He planted his hind end on the ground and stretched both legs out in front of him.

"I'll bring the horses over."

I fetched his pony, Scooty, and Deep, and positioned them so Denny sat in their shadows.

I loosened my shirt around his wrist to let some blood through so he wouldn't get gangrene from lack of circulation.

"How am I doing, brother Will?"

Denny didn't turn his head toward me when he spoke, just his eyes. He sat perfectly still except for his right foot, which wagged back and forth a million times a second.

I reached out my hand and lay it on his ankle.

"Your whole body needs to be still, Denny." His foot stopped, but his eyes opened even wider because all his fear was trapped inside again.

I picked up his hand. It looked good to me; there was just a little blood where I'd cut him. I held the other one up next to it; they were the same size, the same color.

"You're doing a good job, Denny. We're going to sit awhile longer, though, to be sure."

I tightened the tourniquet once more.

"Okay."

As the minutes dragged by, I felt more and more like I might blow into a million pieces. "I'm going to put that shoe back on Deep," I said. "You can watch."

Denny nodded, and his eyes followed me as I pulled my fence pliers and six new nails from one of the saddlebags. I laid the bent heel of the shoe against a big, flat rock. With the rock as my anvil it only took a minute to hammer the heel back flat again with my pliers.

I placed the shoe against Deep's hoof, just slightly off center to the right. I pounded in the first nail on that side, and it went in good and straight, centering the shoe on its way into the hoof, so I pounded the second nail in on the left. I went back and forth, right, left, right, left, until I had the six nails in.

I checked Deep's other feet to make sure all his

shoes had all their nails in good and tight, and then I went back to Denny and knelt down next to him. I picked up both his hands in mine. They were cold and clammy, but they looked the same. I watched his chest; his breathing was regular. The color had come back into his face. My heart leaped; Denny would be fine, he was going to be fine.

I grabbed his shoulders and gave him a shake, I was so happy. He about jumped out of his skin, and his eyes filled up with fearful questions.

"It's okay, Denny! You're going to be fine, just fine. I guess I got all the venom out." I untied my good rodeo shirt.

I smiled at him, and his jack-o'-lantern grin swept over his face, and suddenly, my heart fell. How was I going to get rid of him? But before I could think any more about that, Denny started to bawl. His shoulders hunched and began to bob up and down, and his face got redder and redder as he tried to keep quiet. When I laid my hand on his shoulder real gentle, a sob roared out of him. Both horses shied at the noise, and when I got up to steady them, Denny got louder and louder. I watched him struggle to his feet; he tripped and fell to his hands and knees. He stared at his palms, panting and bleating, and then pushed himself upright again. Tears made muddy tracks down his dusty cheeks. I left the horses and walked toward him, but he ran right past me, hollering, headed back across the land the way he had come.

I stood there staring after him. A little trail of dust followed him across the dry plain. He'd come back once he'd run the fear out of him. Denny always came back.

Denny always came back. Suddenly, a powerful urge grabbed hold of me. It would be the easiest thing in the world. . . . My heart started to pound hard against my ribs. I turned, and I ran so fast toward the horses that Scooty spooked and ran till she saw Deep still standing there not worried a bit. He looked at me with calm, gold-colored eyes.

I slowed myself down, approached Scooty with my hand out, and forced myself to talk slow even though my breath was ragged with huge relief and heavy guilt. I picked up her reins and walked back to Deep, looking around for something to tie her to so she wouldn't follow Deep and me. There was nothing. Nothing.

My eyes flew over the landscape—Denny was still

headed away from me. My eyes swooped back toward the horses and finally lit on my fancy rodeo shirt with Denny's vomit on it. I snatched it up and twirled it back into a tight strand, and I did not let myself think of anything else while I tied one sleeve around Scooty's left front pastern and, leaving about a twelve-inch-length, tied the other sleeve around her right. The hobble was only long enough to let her take short little steps; she would be waiting right there for Denny when he got back.

I looked across the prairie and my heart hammered harder. The dot that was Denny was getting larger.

He had turned.

He was headed back toward me, but slowly.

From my saddlebag I counted out five hard-boiled eggs. That would be plenty of food to see Denny home. I set the food in a neat pile on the ground next to Scooty. Denny would be sure to see it.

My eyes zeroed in on Denny once more. He was still small, still far away. I let out a breath so big it felt like I had been holding it for hours.

I looked around, and my gaze fell on the dead rattler. It'd make good steaks, and I needed to replace the food

I left for Denny. I sharpened my knife on a slab of sandstone, and carefully, holding the rattler behind the head, I cut through the backbone. I kicked the head into the center of a yucca so Denny wouldn't be tempted to touch it again.

I slid my hand down the snake, cut the rattles off, and nestled them amongst the hard-boiled eggs in the saddlebag.

The snake had started to stiffen, but I could still coil it into two loose circles. I used one of the saddle straps to tie it down like an extra rope.

Wet, prickly sweat ran down my neck and sides as I swung into the saddle. I would not look out to see where Denny was. I would not look again. I turned Deep's head toward La Junta, and at the same moment, I leaned forward and pressed my heels hard to his sides.

8

SHORT STACK MOUNTAIN was a tan splotch ten miles or so due north of me. It wavered in the heat, miragelike. I glued my eyes to it and rode Deep hard. I kept him full out for his whole quarter mile and held a steady lope long after that, till the stitch in my side had me almost doubled over.

I slowed up, not wanting to, knowing the slower I went, the faster my brain would work. I kept focused on Short Stack, watching it grow bigger as we approached. It was called Short Stack Mountain because of the way its top had weathered. The wind and rain had worked on it, eroding the softer materials away, and great plates of sandstone were uncovered, so it looked like a short stack of hotcakes piled on top of a big hill. It was a unique enough landmark that folks used it to tell you how far you were from somewhere. Like: "Well, from here it's Short Stack Mountain plus a day east."

A voice in my head nagged that Denny would follow me again. I had counted on his fear and his pain to guarantee my freedom. But his need of me was proving stronger than either.

I looked around, trying to fill my eyes and my head, trying to stop the voice. The land was beginning to roll again, up over mesas sprinkled with junipers and down into canyons sprinkled with junipers.

My need for freedom, for my own life, was stronger than anything. It had to be. *It had to be*. This time, one way or another, I would shake him. For good and for all. I was going to have *my* life, not Denny's life. But how?

In between the mesas and canyons, dry arroyos cut through the landscape, waiting patiently for their streams to come back in.

Somehow I had to make Denny want to go home.

The sun hit the back of my neck just off center; I figured it to be a little past twelve o'clock. I was just a day and a half from La Junta. Short Stack was a mile or so ahead of me; getting there would mean I was only ten or twelve miles short of the Purgatoire River. That's where I would camp for the night, alone.

This first night, the Purgatoire; the next night, I wasn't sure. Before my father had forbidden me to go to the rodeo, he had it set up for me to pass the second night with a doctor friend of his in La Junta. I didn't think that was such a good idea anymore. Could be Hank already contacted Doc Sidder, and he'd be watching for me. I wouldn't take the chance.

Deep and me rode into the shade of Short Stack, and Deep blew as I jumped to the ground, letting me know he was glad for the break. He was hardened off, so he wouldn't need any water till the end of the day when we reached the Purgatoire. During the winter the horses got a little soft because they didn't work so hard. Come spring, we'd start breaking them in to longer and longer spells without water, so by summertime, they could go to the end of a forty- or forty-five-mile riding day with no trouble.

I studied the sky as I stretched my back. I did not look to the south; I could feel Denny out there, but I didn't want to see how close he was.

Thunderheads were rolling my way; it looked like

everybody twenty miles or so to the west was getting hit hard. I felt a current of excitement run through me; how long had it been since I felt rain?

I got out my skinning knife and untied the snake from the saddle. I sat down on the ground and laid the snake out before me. The north side of the hill felt cool to my back. I relaxed against it and fixed my gaze on the headless snake for a minute. He was the color of a summer field drying in the sun. The black splotches were scattered carelessly down his back and each one was just a little different in shape from any of the others. I stroked him, smooth and dry.

Looking at the snake, an idea sparked in my brain; I knew how to make Denny go home! Denny loved presents. Not for themselves, but because they gave him a reason to talk to folks . . . and a way to get folks to listen to him. Presents got people to notice him, and that's what made them irresistible. I shrugged my shoulders to shake off the guilt trying to settle there. It wasn't bribery; it would really just be Denny and me getting what was important to us. Denny would end up back where he belonged, and happy about it, and I would go forward, finally looking out for just myself, finally getting the chance to prove to everybody what kind of hand I was, how good I was at cowboying.

I began to peel the skin back, using my knife tip to cut it free from the tissue inside, rolling it so it was inside out.

Once the skin was off I used the edge of the knife to scrape off the little globs of fat clinging to it, creamy in color, moist, glistening.

I cut off the bottom two-thirds of the skin, and worked it with my fingers to roll it in a bit at a time until it was right side out again. I took my belt off and threaded it through the center of the skin, pressing the moist underside to the leather so it would stick. I stretched it out; it was beautiful. I coiled the fancy new belt and set it on the ground next to me.

At the wide end of the snake I trimmed the patterned skin of his back free from the belly scales and let the piece roll gently in on itself. I wouldn't use it until Denny arrived.

Next, I picked up the carcass again and, cutting and pulling, peeled the meat off the ribs on each side until there were two strips about three and a half feet long, about an inch wide and a half-inch thick. I cut two good-size steaks from one of them and rubbed salt over the rest so it wouldn't spoil. There was room in the saddlebag for all the meat.

A few minutes later I had a small fire popping and crackling, built from dried-up little bluestem grass and dead cholla. The sweet, pink rattler steaks sizzled in my small fry pan; a smile crept onto my lips. It felt good to fend for myself, like stretching a cramped muscle.

9

THE SOUND OF SCOOTY'S hooves pounding toward me pricked at my ears like a crow at carrion, and my pride in providing for myself took on a bitter edge. I had been unable to outrun my hunter. My only chance for escape was to outwit him.

The wind kicked up and swirled in different directions, and thunder drummed behind the mountains. I took a deep breath, slapped my knees, and pushed myself to my feet. I turned to face my stalker when I heard his gasping and snorting.

Denny sat on Scooty, shaking his snakebit hand down by his side, and clutching my rodeo shirt up on his chest with the other.

"Hi. Hi, brother Will! Here is your shirt." Denny

waved my fancy rodeo shirt in the air. His eyes were sprung wide; he was talking fast, so spit was flying. "You forgot it. It was on Scooty's legs."

I shook my head; it took a lot of hard thinking for him to see my shirt could be his excuse to follow me.

Denny lowered his head and looked me dead in the eye. He looked sly and proud.

"Get down and come eat dinner." I would not start explaining. I would go forward.

Denny thudded to the ground and caught his breath. His legs had been straight when his feet hit the hard earth; his joints would be so stiff after riding so far that they would hardly bend. Even a couple miles on horseback made Denny limp, and he'd done twenty miles in one day.

I saw him wince and blink back tears, but "I'm hungry, brother Will," was all he said.

"Did you eat the eggs I left?"

"They were way back there." Denny pointed south.

"They were enough to get you home. You would've had your dinner by now if you'd gone back to the ranch." I made myself stop; telling Denny what he should have done just made him stubborn. "Here." I tossed my skinning knife to the ground at his feet. "Go cut a juniper branch; I don't have any extra silverware."

"I could not go home, brother Will. You forgot your shirt. I told that to you. You forgot your rodeo shirt."

Denny waved my shirt again, picked up my knife, and stumbled over to the closest juniper. He kept nodding at me while he stuck his arms into the center and trimmed off a stem. He was hoping if he nodded long enough, I'd agree with him. I stuck the fork hard into the steaks to flip them and set the fry pan at the edge of the fire.

I stripped all the green side twigs off the juniper bough and speared my steak. I handed Denny the tin plate and silverware. We were both silent while we ate. When I looked down at my food, or when I looked out to the weather headed our way, from the corner of my eye I saw Denny lower his head and pull in his cheeks and stare at me. In his way, he was plotting and planning, biding his time, just as I was.

"Denny?" I swallowed the last of the rattlesnake. "I need to talk to you about something serious."

Denny's eyes narrowed. He started shaking that snakebit hand again.

"I'm going to the rodeo, Denny."

"I know that."

"You are going home."

Denny shook his head hard. "No. I am not going home, brother Will. I am going with you. I can help. I will bemember things for you. Like I bemembered your rodeo shirt. After the rodeo, then I'll go home. We can go home together."

I felt muscles harden through my whole body like I was going to hit something. My face was hot; I was hot all over.

"Denny, I am going out to start my grown-up life. I'm not going back home. I'm not going back."

My words came out in a loud rush; they had never been out in the air before.

Denny's eyes were stretched too wide; he looked like he might drown.

"No. No, no, no, no!" He yelled louder with each word. "You are not a grown-up, brother Will. You are not going away to be grown-up. You are going to the rodeo." Denny pushed himself to stand, kicking up dust with his scrambling boots. "Nobody has talked about this."

I kept my seat. I took in a long, slow breath and let

it seep out of me. "When you are grown-up, you don't have to talk to other people about your plans. You make a plan, and you carry it out, Denny. That's all I'm doing. I am going to win first place in the La Junta Rodeo, and then I am going to hire on with another ranch, and then I am going to Wyoming for the big rodeo there. That is my plan."

"But, brother Will"—Denny's voice quavered, his cheeks bunched up—"I don't have a plan. Nobody said I would need a plan." Fat tears spilled out of his eyes.

My throat tightened, my eyes burned. My heart thumped against my ribs.

It was as though I was walking on wet, slippery stones at the edge of Pacheco's Water Hole.

I forced my brain to think, to give me a picture, and I saw me and Denny on the ranch forever.

Denny never grown.

Me never grown.

I pushed out a short, harsh breath.

"Denny, your plan is to go home, go back to the ranch. That's where your work is. You know Father counts on you to collect the eggs every day and do the sweeping; you have lots of responsibilities."

I was slow and gentle. I was shrewd.

"Denny, I have a present for you—actually, two."

I saw a spark come to Denny's eyes. He drew muddy streaks down his cheeks with the back of his hands.

"I made some fancy things from the rattlesnake for you to show everybody back home. That way, they'll believe you when you tell the big story about getting bit by a dead rattler."

I reached for the coiled belt and knocked my hand against my canteen, tipping it. Quick-like, I tossed the belt to Denny so I could save my day's water.

It was not until I heard him yelp and looked up to see cold fear rush over his face that I realized what I'd done. I wished I could pull the belt back, but all I could do was put my arm around Denny.

"I'm sorry, Denny. Sorry." I bent down and picked the belt off the ground. "I skinned the snake and made him into a belt for you. See? Want to try it on?"

Denny slowly reached his hand out to the belt, stroked it with his index finger. "Oh, brother Will . . . it is beautiful, huh. The spots and the smooth." Denny looked up at me. "This belt is for me? You made this for me, brother Will?"

My stomach did a roll, my jaw clenched down; all I could do was nod. I looked away for a minute.

I cleared my throat; I would go forward.

I was going to have my life.

I watched him whip his old belt off. He tossed it to me with a big jack-o'-lantern grin. "Here. Catch *my* snake." He threaded his new belt through the loops on his pants; he would miss the one in the center back. When he went to fasten the buckle his tongue would poke out the right side of his mouth to help him concentrate.

"Denny," I said, and turned my back so I didn't have to watch. I picked up the rolled piece of snakeskin from the ground. "I have another present for you. Something else to show Hank and the rest of the boys when you get back to the ranch this evening."

"I can show the presents after the rodeo, brother Will. I can show Hank and the boys when we go home. Together. That way they will believe in my story." A question was in his eyes; he was testing, testing.

I shook my head. "No, Denny. These are presents for you to take back with you today. If you don't go home, you don't get to keep the presents."

Denny's lower jaw jutted out, and his eyes narrowed. "Well, then, what is the other present? This is a skinny belt. I will still go to the rodeo."

I felt my own eyes narrow. I shook my head. "Come here." I walked over to Scooty and unrolled the skin. "See this?"

I made myself take a deep breath. I had to be calm. "It's a decoration for the cantle of your saddle."

I laid it up close to the cantle so he could see how good it would look, but I didn't stick it on yet.

"Nobody else has one of these. You'll be the only one. Why, anytime anyone sees your saddle they'll want to hear the story behind it. Think of it, Denny, always able to tell your rattlesnake story and somebody always wanting to hear it."

"Somebody would always want to listen, huh, brother Will?"

I saw strong hunger creep into Denny's eyes from the bottom up. I had him; the knot tightened in my gut.

10

MILES AND TIME wandered past me and Deep. A cool wind was running over the Sangre de Cristos, racing with the rain clouds. Deep was frisking up. He pressed forward into his brow band, picked his knees up.

"Okay," I said. "Let's go."

I tried to lift my spirits as I lifted my voice. I loosened up on the reins so Deep broke into an easy lope. But I could not shake the picture of Denny, arms hung by his side, eyes staring at his blood-spattered boots. I had tried to think of something to make it easier.

"Tell you what," I said. "You like getting mail, don't you? You like it when Aunt Gladys sends the birthday cards and the letter at Christmastime, don't you? Here's what. I'll write to you every week. Or every couple weeks. I promise, Denny."

But he just stared at his boots.

"You head home now, brother Denny. I'll see you in two Christmases. Tell everybody about the rattlesnake, okay? Show them the belt and your saddle. Okay? Just ride back to the mesa, around the mesa, and you'll be home. Okay?"

I stepped forward and put my arms around Denny. His arms hung, he stared at his boots. I squeezed my arms around him and stepped back. I stared down at my own boots. A drop fell on the left one. A tear. I don't know if it was mine or Denny's.

At late afternoon Deep and me stood on the rim of the canyon, four hundred feet above the Purgatoire River. Raindrops pelted me as I fished my slicker out of the saddlebag. Even so far above the river I could see it was running high and swift for July. The clouds must have dumped a lot of their water upstream.

I started Deep down a game trail, a narrow one without much room for mistakes. Not one to try any but the steadiest horse on. A startle or even a short skid sideways could tip you off the edge. We passed between junipers and chollas. The rain was falling heavy, and we took it real slow; little rivulets ran down the trail and made it slick.

The thunder and lightning cracked and flashed right over our heads. The sound was deafening; it blocked Denny from my thoughts, stopped me from thinking about what I'd done. I was grateful for it. The sky was dark and heavy looking; I could smell hail about to start. A roadrunner raced across the trail down in front of us, his neck stretched out long, almost parallel to the ground, trying to get home quick so the paint on his feathers didn't run. A loud clap of thunder, and I flinched; Deep didn't miss a beat. He held his head low against the rain and kept on.

The hail unloaded all at once, and the footing became even more treacherous. The ice balls were marble-size, and their pelts stung my hands.

The trail started to level out and widen as we approached the bottom of the canyon. It was a good thing, as Deep was now slinging his head trying to avoid the hailstones.

I got popped on the last knuckle of my right index

finger. The ice was so sharp it cut the skin; blood trickled down my palm.

We were moving through willow thickets now that we were down close to the river, and they snagged the side flaps of my slicker, shredding little pieces from it. I felt miserable; Deep probably did too.

Finally, we made it down to the river's edge, and the roar of the water muffled the thunder. The water was muddy, churning, several feet wider and deeper than normal in the summer. White water careened around and over the boulders in the middle.

Normally this stretch of the Purgatoire didn't run more than a foot or foot and a half deep. Now some of the smaller bushes at the edge were half-submerged; the water had to be up over three feet, close to chest high on Deep.

I turned to flip my saddlebags up onto Deep's rump so they wouldn't get drenched when we crossed, and as I did my eye caught movement back up the trail.

I swiped the rain from my eyes, not believing, not wanting to. My breath caught in my throat as I looked again.

Scooty was sliding straight-legged down the path

through the mud and the hail. Denny was lying back in the saddle, almost horizontal, clawing at the saddle horn, trying to get a grip. Only his head was up. His hair was plastered, soaking wet to his head. His face was twisted, his mouth was wide open, but I could not hear the screams.

Cold fear streaked through me. I wheeled Deep back toward Denny and urged him hard up the trail.

I peered through the sheeting rain, filled with dread.

But there was Scooty, still upright on all four hooves, and there was Denny, clinging tight to the saddle horn. And I realized, even if Scooty went down, even if Denny fell, they were close enough now to the bottom of the canyon that he'd be okay. He'd be safe.

I leaned heavily on the pommel of my saddle, weak with relief, and suddenly dizzy as it dawned on me that finally, *finally*, Denny was at a dead end. Distance hadn't stopped him, pain hadn't turned him back, but the river would. The water would. He might ride right to the river's edge, but he would never enter into that deep, dark water. Water that he could drown in, be lost in, the same as Momma. He would turn, defeated, and go home.

I watched a moment longer, sucked in a ragged breath, and then I turned Deep away, down toward the river. I guided him into the churning water, letting him have his head so he could find his own footing, and I locked my eyes onto the far bank.

The hail had shrunk to pea-size, and it didn't hurt nearly as bad when it pinged off my skin. It was slowing down some, too, and dropped softly into the river, forming bright, white circles before the current found them and sent them spinning on.

Above us the sky was still dark, and the lightning flashed orange and mean-looking, but I heard no thunder, no screaming, only the rushing water that surrounded us, turning Deep into an island.

We were just about midway, at the river's deepest point. I rode with my feet forward of the stirrups, trying to keep my boots from filling, for the water was up between Deep's chest and the point of his shoulder. Deep picked his way thoughtfully, lifting his knees high, setting his feet down softly, then slowly settling his weight, making sure of his footing. Every so often I felt the river push him and felt him brace into it.

I saw we'd be able to come out at a nice, low spot on

the bank. My gaze traveled up the river, over its soft bends and curves. And then suddenly, my eyes slammed into something dark and huge roiling down the channel like a locomotive. I stared, my mind clamoring for an explanation, a definition. It looked almost like a storm cloud, but solid, and suddenly I understood that the black, surging wall was water; a flash flood had hit the Purgatoire, and it was fast pushing toward us.

Instinctively, I moved my heels to Deep's sides to spur him forward, and then, instinctively, I halted the movement. With dread, unable to stop myself, I turned back over my shoulder to be sure of Denny.

Scooty was in the river. Crossing the river. Her ears were laid flat to her head, her eyes rolled back in panic, showing the whites. She was trying to jump through the swirling water to reach Deep.

I pulled hard on the reins so that Deep stopped and then, unwillingly, started to back. Four hesitating steps.

Denny was thrown forward over the saddle horn, hanging off Scooty's right side. His arms were clamped around her neck. His eyes were stretched wide; his mouth was a gaping hole. And suddenly, I could hear his screams.

I watched the solid wave of water ignore the

meanderings of the channel and blast straight for us.

Another step back. Dark as death, it was not like water at all.

Deep was tossing his head, fighting the bit. He knew we were going the wrong way. I extended my right arm behind me, out of the shoulder socket, toward Scooty's reins.

Denny was screaming, Scooty was squealing. My hand stretched, my bones were going to bust through the skin at my fingertips. My hand closed on Scooty's wet reins, and at the same moment I slid my left hand back on Deep's, giving him his head, and I dug my heels into his ribs and prayed.

It startled him, and he lunged forward, his hooves slipped over rocks, and I was flung forward onto his neck. Seconds seemed to take days. I saw the opposite bank six feet ahead. My eyes locked onto the heaving wall of water, and as it roared closer, I saw eddies swirling within it. I was mesmerized by the tumbling shapes until I realized it wasn't just spinning water I saw, but spinning trout, helpless against the water's force.

"No!" I heard myself yell.

I wouldn't be taken. I'd fought too hard already to

have it all end the same as it had for Momma. I urged Deep forward with a sharp kick and felt his front legs pull up onto the bank and then his back legs. My right arm was yanked hard as Scooty bent her legs trying to jump to land, and her reins ripped from my hand.

Before I could turn, I heard Denny scream, and the water rushed past me with the force of a twister.

11

I GOT OFF DEEP WITH my eyes shut. I felt soggy ground beneath my feet, and my ears were filled with the sound of the flood crashing on. I leaned my forehead against Deep's neck and breathed in his wet, horsey smell until my heart slowed.

Then I opened my eyes and turned, prepared to see nothing behind me. But Scooty was there on the bank, legs spread, shaking the water off. Denny was there too.

He was flat on his back, his face ghost-white. His shirt was ripped; his chest and belly were red. Bloody.

I ran to him and saw his eyes were open. The rain bounced off his face and streamed into his eyes; he stared unblinking at the sky.

"Oh, Denny! Brother Denny." I knelt beside him,

my face close to his, and I saw his lips move. I turned my head so my ear was almost against his mouth; my heart thundered with the fear that these might be Denny's last words. I was drowning in my thoughts; I should have taken Denny home, made sure he was safe. I should have dived deeper in the pool and pulled Momma up.

There was only the roar of the river and the flood of guilt. I pressed my hands against his cheeks. "Denny, Denny."

There. But so soft.

"What, Denny? What?"

"I did, I did . . ." His voice trailed off; I couldn't make sense of it.

"What is it, Denny? I couldn't hear; what is it?" I was panicked; I had to know what he meant, what he wanted. "Denny. Come on, Denny, try again."

"I made the . . ." His voice was so weak, it seemed like he was having a hard time getting air.

"Okay, Denny," I said. "Take it easy. Just try one more time."

He was silent for so long I began to tremble, and then I saw him struggle to gather his strength.

"What, Denny?"

He sighed. He squeezed his eyes tight and sat up. "I made it," he said. "I crossed the river, brother Will. I did it!"

I rocked back on my heels. I looked at him, his bangs separated into ribbons on his forehead, water dripping from his chin. His slanty blue eyes were dancing, every one of his pointed teeth showed, his grin was ear to ear. He stuck out his left hand.

"Let's shake on it. On the good job I did. This is more better than the snake story."

I stared at Denny for a moment, feeling nothing, blank, like the river had scoured me clean. And then something deep inside me, something rigid and brittle, started to twist. I almost heard it when it snapped. I felt it, that's for sure, and it snapped so hard and so quick it sent me staggering to my feet. I had felt this part of me writhe and strain and groan before, but now it had broken, and I didn't know what would happen.

Suddenly, words I had never let myself think spewed out of my mouth like rattlesnake venom.

"You goddurned moron!" I yelled. "I hate you, Denny. I hate you. You hear me?"

Denny's mouth fell open, his eyes filled with surprise and then pain; and I wanted to hurt him more.

I reached out and grabbed his shirt collar in both my hands, and I dragged him to his feet. I held him with my left hand, and I punched him in the face with my right.

I punched him again, and he didn't raise a hand to stop me.

He bleated and sobbed.

And suddenly, I was sobbing too. I yanked my hand off his collar, and Denny slumped to the ground. He rolled away from me, his hands over his face.

My arms dropped, limp, to my sides. My knees shook. I lowered myself onto a rock. I was still crying. Silently. The roaring river was all the sound in the world.

I didn't know how much time had passed when I finally started to notice things again. I saw the horses grazing on the low part of the canyon wall, the river surging on, over its banks. The huge wave was gone, but the Purgatoire had swallowed up all the saplings and bushes and boulders that stood four or five feet off her banks. The landscape was emptier. The world had changed so fast, so unexpectedly; my sense of time was mixed up, and I suddenly wondered if it hadn't happened so quick after all, and instead I'd been sitting there for years.

My eyes rushed to find Denny to reassure myself. He was rolled into a tight, silent ball right where I dropped him. His hands still covered his face. His trunk was still bloody. *Bloody.*

"Denny!" My heart started to pound, and I ran to him. I had to force his arms apart so I could see his injuries; but he wouldn't uncover his face. His shirt was ripped, his belly and chest scraped and bruised, but none of it looked deep. Probably he fell off Scooty and hit a rock when she jumped onto the bank.

"Denny? You okay, Denny?"

He didn't move or speak. He did not want me to see him, and he did not want to see me.

"Denny, it's getting late. We need to get to higher ground and settle in; it'll be dark before long."

He didn't move. He didn't speak.

My right hand was so sore I could hardly bear to close it, but I gripped his wrists tight.

I didn't want him to see me. I didn't want to see him.

Finally, I made myself pull his hands away from his

face. I flinched, dropped my hold.

Denny's left eyelid and cheek were swelled, so his eye was open only a slit. The deep purple bruise underneath made my stomach turn over. His right cheek was pulpy and dark too.

My breath caught in my throat; I looked away. I scooped up a handful of hail. "Sit up, Denny," I said. "Close your eye all the way and then put this ice on it. On your other cheek too. I'll get the horses."

I turned his hand palm up and dumped the hail into it and then stood, turning my back to Denny's damaged face, but it was too late. What I'd done wasn't only on his face; it was inside both of us.

I fetched my canteen and went down to the river to refill it and then reached my hurt hand deep into the foaming Purgatoire and splashed its icy water over my face again and again until the ache left my fingers and my face was numb. I took a long draught from the canteen.

I watered the horses three times, letting them have just a moderate amount each time so they wouldn't overdrink and bloat after the long day of riding.

At last I walked back to Denny and handed him the

canteen. When he was finished drinking I filled it again, then led Scooty over to him and handed him the reins. He did not look at me; he did not speak to me.

I climbed on Deep and started up the canyon wall. When I looked back, Denny was still sitting on the ground.

"Denny, come on. Let's get up to the rim."

Slowly, he stood and pulled himself onto Scooty's back.

As we climbed higher we left the angry roar of the Purgatoire below us, and the world began to feel familiar and safe in the sunset. The sky was clearing to a soft, faded blue, and the clouds out to the west were fading pink and golden and couldn't hurt a flea.

We hauled up onto the rim of the canyon; four ferruginous hawks glided above us, their underbellies pure white. They soared in a great circle as though enjoying each other's company while they waited for a rabbit to show up.

The world was just as wet on top as it was down below, and there was no chance I'd get a fire started. I took my bedroll apart and threw the three blankets over a couple junipers so the breeze could dry them. I took off my soaking clothes and spread them over another bush. Denny sat on Scooty.

"You need to get out of your wet clothes, Denny. Throw them over a bush like I did so they'll dry."

Denny lumbered down, grunting in pain when his legs hit the ground straight. He started to fiddle with his shirt buttons, but then saw the fabric was ripped all the way down. He slid the shirt off, lay it carefully over a juniper while I unsaddled the horses.

The food had kept fairly dry in the saddlebags; I divvied up a dozen hard-boiled chicken eggs, some jerky, and half a bread loaf for each of us.

Denny did not talk to me. He did not look at me, not even when I stared off into the distance and gave him the chance.

The peace of the evening settled over us. The sky darkened, and a pale moon was on the rise. The breeze was soft; it lifted my hair gently. I breathed in slow and deep and breathed out some of the day's fear, some of the day's blackness.

I pulled the blankets down from the bush; they were mostly dry. I laid two of the blankets together, folded them in half, and smoothed them out on the ground.

"Denny, time for sleep. This'll be your bedroll."

Denny shuffled over, wiggled between the layers.

"Denny, take your boots off."

He tugged them off, lay back down.

He did not look at me. He did not speak.

I shimmied in between the halves of my folded blanket. Darkness was coming on real gentle; it seeped into me, softening my bones, softening my heart. "We were lucky today, Denny. It may not seem exactly like that, but we were plain lucky." I tried a chuckle. "I just hope we don't have to be lucky tomorrow. It wore me out."

Denny did not speak.

I lay quiet for a time, until the moon was high and bright as it would get. I could see the outlines of junipers and horses and the hump of Denny's knees. I sat up and tapped on them until I saw him turn his head toward me, and then, in the darkness, where I couldn't see his eyes, in the darkness where he couldn't see mine, I made a cross of my index fingers and pressed them to my heart.

12

THE SUN HADN'T BEGUN to show, the sky was still gray, when Denny's snoring and the squawk of the scrub jays woke me. I pushed myself up to sit in the cool morning air, pulled the scratchy blanket over my shoulders. I looked out to the east. The plain was wide and empty; it was a world where there was only the future.

Everything seemed different suddenly, on the far side of the Purgatoire. I had crossed not just a river, but also a line. A line that separated me from what was familiar, separated me from the past. My past.

Before I could stop it, a picture washed into my head: the circle of blue sky edged by rock walls and scrub oak that was all I could see when I was far down

Cobert Canyon lying on a sun-warmed rock. A terrible longing came on the heels of the image.

A longing for home.

A longing for Momma. For all the places she loved. For all the places on the ranch I could still picture her.

Denny let out a snort and rolled toward me. I studied his face. Both cheeks were puffy and purple. His eye was a little less swollen. I thought he should be able to open it all right.

What about Denny? He had crossed the Purgatoire, too. But I had to get him back to the ranch. That was where he belonged, where he'd be happy.

Envy crept into my empty stomach: Denny could be happy on the ranch.

The sun was a skinny little edge inching above the horizon now, and the ravens started their raucous morning calls.

I took a deep breath that left no room for the gall in my belly. Denny was a boy; I was a man. I pulled on my dry socks and boots and visited a pile of rocks before I dressed. I started whistling and made myself keep on.

We were forty miles from home, and that was too far for Denny to travel safely alone. Especially with the river between him and the ranch.

There was nothing for it but to go on together. That way I'd be able to make sure he ended up safe; I felt a weight lift. I whistled louder.

The three-awn grass that was everywhere made good kindling for my fire, and I kicked out a distance beyond camp to hunt some dry cholla and juniper wood.

Denny's snoring quit about the time the fire started to crackle, but he didn't admit to being awake until the coffee was ready.

"What will happen now, Will?"

His voice was quiet as he tugged on his pants and boots. When he sat down I handed him the first cup of coffee. I waited to speak; where was the "brother Will"?

"What will happen today, Will?"

I took a quick glance at him, trying to figure, but all I saw were the bruises.

"We'll get to La Junta, or the outskirts, by late afternoon," I said. "Around suppertime, and we'll set up camp on the western edge of town."

"Don't I have to go home, Will?"

I paused once more, listening for "brother Will," but it didn't come.

"You'd have to cross the river again. The water's probably down, but you'd still have to do it alone. Do you want to, Denny?"

He was quiet for a minute. "Uh-uh."

"Well then, we'll do like I said."

Camping outside town would be safer than going into La Junta. I did not want to chance running into Doc Sidder and having him corner me. I would've bet either my father or Hank had called him by then and told him to keep an eye out for me, for us.

"Tomorrow morning after breakfast we'll ride to the rodeo grounds, eyeball the stock. The first event goes on at ten. As soon as I'm done, as soon as I claim the first place winnings—" My palms were suddenly moist; I stood up too quick, slopping coffee into the fire and making it spit. I *will* get first place. I *have* to get first.

"Well then, I'll call home and set up a place for them to pick you up, you and Scooty."

"What about you, Will?"

"I'll stay out of sight until I see somebody show up for you, and then I guess I'll move on. I'll spend some time after the rodeo talking to the stock handlers and ranch foremen to see who will pay me best, and then that's where I'll go."

"Won't you say good-bye?"

"Sure I'll say good-bye to you, Denny."

Denny shook his head. "No. Good-bye to our dad, or good-bye to Hank."

"If I did that, either one of them would likely try to drag me back home."

Denny was silent for a long minute. He looked me hard in the eyes, drawing his cheeks in, and said, "Grown-ups do like they want. There is nobody that makes them."

13

We rode a couple of hours in silence. The country that stretched before us was arid, not from short-term drought, but from long-term geography and wind patterns. It was even drier than the ranch. Yucca, sagebrush, rattlesnakes, and cholla cactus were its specialties. Denny and I had always called it *jumping* cholla because no matter how wide a berth we gave it, we'd still end up with spines in our pant legs or our shirts by the end of the day.

We were probably just six or seven when we had our first run-in with jumping cholla. We were out riding bareback on a little painted pony, coming down the mesa, headed for home one evening. The pony was spooky by nature, and when a roadrunner danced in front of her she began to jump and rear. We both went flying, and we ended up knocking heads when we came to rest in a good-size batch of cholla. I crashed belly-first through at least six of them before I hit the ground.

Even as bad as it hurt I had to get up quick. The weight of my body pushed all those needles in deeper every second. I hauled Denny onto his feet; every little movement pushed or pulled on a pricker and kept us both whimpering.

Straight-legged so my jeans wouldn't rub so bad on the spines in my legs, I walked down the hill to where the paint grazed. That durn horse looked like she'd been standing there the whole day, peaceful as could be. Man, I wanted to kick her, but if she ran off, we'd have a mile and a half to walk to home.

I picked up her reins, and I couldn't help screaming out when I hauled myself onto her back. Denny let out a howl when I pulled him up behind me; and we both bawled all the way home.

"What is funny, Will?"

When I heard Denny's voice I realized I had been a million miles away. "I was thinking about the time that paint bucked us off into the cholla."

"Yowch."

"Yeah. Remember Momma got out her best tweezers?"

"Yowch. It took a very long time. There was lots of stickers."

"She didn't get them all. I have a patch on my wrist that's red even now. It feels like sandpaper; it still tingles sometimes."

"I have got that too. On my knee."

14

BLACK CLOUDS TRAILED us from the Sangre de Cristos, and thunder rumbled in the background, threatening. But it was not loud or insistent enough to distract me from Denny's snakebit hand. It was infected. I'd taken a close look at it when we stopped to rest Denny's hips. The skin around the fang puncture was puffy and red, and it felt warmer than the skin further out.

Rain began to fall; small drops splattered on the ground and made the air smell of dust.

When I was planning this trip my father had told me about a creek north of La Junta where I could water Deep before spending the night at Doc Sidder's in town that second night. I was hoping the stream had a strong flow so I could wash out Denny's bite real good. If not, I'd have to just use canteen water. Then I'd bandage it up and see if it wasn't better the next morning. Denny said it wasn't sore, but I knew it was. I turned back and looked at him on Scooty, feeling irritated. He was holding his infected hand curled on his thigh.

"Your hand hurts, doesn't it, Denny?"

"Uh-uh."

"Why do you always have to say things don't hurt? You know it hurts, and I know it hurts."

Denny didn't say anything; I turned my back to him. Several minutes passed.

"The same reason as you."

"What?" I turned to look at him again. He didn't even blink as he stared back at me.

"When a something hurts. I don't say about it just like you don't."

"I say when something hurts, Denny."

"Our red cowboy boots."

"What?"

"Red cowboy boots. The ones Momma got for us."

Man. I hadn't thought of those boots, well, probably since I outgrew them. They were Momma's present to us for our fifth birthday. They were beauts, too. The leather on the sides was dyed red, and there was a dark blue panel that ran all the way up the middle of them. They pinched like the devil right from the start, but I was so proud of those boots, so taken with them, I wasn't about to quit wearing them.

Denny didn't say a word, either, about how they rubbed, but long about day five or six, Momma noticed we'd both developed a limp. She tugged our boots off and had a fit when she saw all the raw, red blisters we had. But she was even more troubled by the smell; we were in a lot deeper when she finally got us to confess we'd been putting them back on before we got into bed at night and sleeping in them.

I turned to Denny, smiling, but the smug look on his face made me face frontward again. He was thinking how smart he was to prove me wrong. A sigh and a realization built inside of me. When we were small Denny and I did everything together. And things were the same for us both; we had the same experience. We both got bucked into the cholla and ended up full of spines; we both got blisters from our birthday boots and got in trouble the same. We both got paddled for sneaking the barn cat into the house and feeding him the chicken livers Momma had set aside for turkey dressing.

How long had it been since Denny and I did something together that was the same for us both?

15

THE STORM THAT HAD been dogging us all day was moving off to the southeast, and the sun had that late afternoon sear to it; you could've fried a steak on the back of my neck. I could just pick out the town of La Junta huddled out to the east and looking small with green fields of sugar beets and melons surrounding it, maybe five miles beyond us. And that meant the creek should be showing up in another mile or two. I scanned the landscape for green, and I spotted cottonwood trees, a sure sign of water. We didn't have any cottonwoods close to the ranch or the mesa; they were water guzzlers and couldn't take our dry conditions.

I swung a little more to the north to cut our distance to the creek and turned to tell Denny we were almost there. As soon as our eyes met he jerked his sore hand out from where he had it tucked under his other arm and laid it, still curled, back on his thigh.

"La Junta," I said.

"Okay."

I noticed, too, how tall he was sitting in the saddle; his back must have ached from the long ride and Scooty's rough trot.

We were about an eighth of a mile away when Deep smelled water and picked up his pace. When we got to the creek it was all I could do to get him to stay put long enough to unsaddle him. He walked to the edge of the creek and blew before he started sucking it up.

Denny let Scooty walk into the creek with him, which surprised me, but I didn't have time to comment because she decided to take a roll with Denny still on her back.

"Jump!" I yelled. "She'll roll over on you if you let her go down."

But Scooty was already on her knees in the water; Denny was on her far side, scrunched way down like a dwarf and hopping on one foot. His other foot was caught in the stirrup.

I splashed into the creek, spooking Deep, which in turn spooked Scooty. She scrambled back to her feet, water pouring off her, and Denny fell down hard on his backside. His foot was free.

I kept running, worried Denny was going to panic being in water. But he called out to me, and it stopped me short.

"There is not too much water. It feels good on my hand."

When I told Denny to lead Scooty out of the water so she didn't overdrink, I saw he did it with his good hand, and when I asked him to help me scare up firewood, he carried it back in his arms so his infected hand didn't bear any weight. I had to look at it. I had been leaving it, hoping a good soaking in the creek would bring some of the swelling down, turn it into a small thing.

"Come over here, Denny. I need to look at your hand."

"I think it is fine." Denny stumbled on the rocks and twigs as he shuffled over. He plunked down beside me and stuck his hand under my nose.

It wasn't fine; the bite was more swollen than it had

been at noontime, and there was a yellow cast to the skin; there must have been a fair amount of pus under there. The red area was larger too, and Denny's first three fingers and his thumb were puffy at their bases.

I looked closer and cursed; creeping out from the bite itself were two short, parallel, red lines. Denny's hand wasn't only infected; he had blood poisoning.

My throat tightened; Denny needed a doctor and medicine. And he needed them both quick, before those red lines started up his arm toward his heart. I would have to take him into La Junta, and it was unlikely that there would be more than one doctor in town. I had to take Denny to see my father's friend, Doc Sidder.

My heart pounded. What if my father had talked to the doctor and told him if I showed up not to let me go? I could just leave Denny on his doorstop and knock and run. But they'd know I was there; they could hunt me down before the rodeo.

I wiped my palms on my jeans. My brain raced, searching for another way. There was something my father told me once, something that could cure blood poisoning. He used it when he got blood poisoning from a boil, and it worked. Coneflower is what it was. I looked around. There was no coneflower; there was only Denny sitting with his infected hand tucked protectively under his other arm, Denny rocking back and forth.

16

"DING-DONG."

"Stop it, Denny."

Denny reached out and pushed the black doorbell again.

"That is a happy sound. It is fun for my ears. Ding-dong."

We were waiting on the front porch of Doc Sidder's frame house. It was set in the middle of a block, and all the houses looked alike. But hanging from the ceiling of his porch was a wooden shingle that was painted up fancy, with two wings at its top and two snakes wrapped around a pole below. That let people know there was a medical man inside.

"Will." Denny's head was tilted back; his jaw hung as

he looked at the top of the house. "This house is different. From yours or mine. Somebody painted it. The house is white everywhere. Our house at home is made of rocks. Cool sumbertime. Warm winter. Our dad says that, Will."

Denny pointed his index finger at the doorbell again, and I grabbed it away just as the door swung open.

A middle-aged man stood before us wearing city duds: pressed brown trousers, a starched white shirt. There were no mended holes anywhere on his clothes. Gold-framed eyeglasses set low on his nose.

"Dr. Sidder?"

He looked me over from the crown of my hat to the toes of my boots. His eyes moved to Denny and narrowed as they came to rest on his black eye.

I felt sweat spring up on my forehead.

"You Gil Bennon's boys?"

Denny sat on the chair in Doc Sidder's examining room, his body rigid, his cheeks sucked in. The doctor turned Denny's hand over, prodding and poking at the red, taut skin.

"You were right to come in. And you were right in your diagnosis; it's blood poisoning. Come tomorrow Dennis would have spiked a fever and begun to feel fluish. Harder to manage the further along it gets, too, just like anything else." He crossed to the deep metal sink and washed his hands.

"So, he's going to be all right?"

"He is. I've got the right medicine for it."

"Coneflower?"

Doc Sidder looked at me over his eyeglasses. "Learn that from your dad?"

I nodded.

"That's an old Indian cure for blood poisoning. Works pretty well, if you catch it in time. But we have something better now."

He walked over to a glass cabinet filled with brown glass jars, and picked one up. From the bottle he shook two white tablets into his hand.

"It's called sulfanilamide. A German fellow discovered it four or five years ago. It's taken this long to get it over the pond and all the way out West. Kills germs." Doc Sidder ran the cold tap at the sink and filled a glass. "Dennis, do you know how to take a pill?"

Denny's eyebrows raised high. "No one says 'Dennis' to me. Why do you know 'Dennis'?"

Doc Sidder gave a small smile. "I know your brother's name too. It's Willard."

Denny was delighted; his mouth broke out in a toothy grin. "Ha!"

A nervous tingle shot through my shoulders and my arms; I was uncomfortable with how much Doc Sidder seemed to know about us. I wanted to be careful. I felt like a coyote that had just spotted a trap sticking out from under a pile of leaves.

"I've known your father for twenty-five years. Knew your mother, too. Here." Doc Sidder handed the glass to Denny. "Take a drink of the water, then put the pill on your tongue, take more water, and swallow it down."

I saw the confusion on Denny's face. "He'll do better one step at a time," I said to the doctor. "Take a drink, Denny, and swallow it." I directed Denny in pill swallowing and felt Doc Sidder studying me all the while.

Denny got the pill down, but gave a shudder and made a face. "Bluh," he said.

"Come over to the sink so we can get that bite cleaned out. I'll use that same medicine in a powder directly on the wound."

Doc Sidder turned on a small, bright lamp that set on the counter next to the sink. Denny shuffled over. The doctor reached out and took Denny's chin in one hand, and with the other he tilted the light so it shone on Denny's bruises.

"What happened to your cheek and your eye, son?"

Denny looked past the light to me, locked his eyes with mine until I looked away.

There was a long silence. I felt Doc Sidder's gaze weighing me down; my chest was tight with guilt.

"Dennis? What happened to your face?" he asked a little louder.

"I got poked."

"Poked, huh? With what?"

"We got into a fight," I said. "Or I got into a fight. I got angry."

"The crossing the river was hard."

"Mm. Does your brother get angry very often, Dennis?"

My legs and my arms felt like they were shriveling up with shame.

"Nope."

"Good." Doc Sidder turned his gaze on me. I forced my eyes not to shift away, and I forced my throat not to swallow.

"You boys will have quite a tale to tell when you get home."

"Willard is not going home."

I heard myself suck in my breath. Doc Sidder heard me suck in my breath; and I wanted to kick myself and strangle Denny for giving so much away. I glared at Denny, started to shake my head to signal him not to talk anymore, but Doc Sidder's eyes were on me again.

"Not going home, eh? What are your plans, Willard?"

I could smell the metal of the trap all tangy; I could feel the tension of its spring in the long bones of my legs. I knew it would snap any second, but I could not help stretching my muzzle out toward it; I could not help taking one more step.

"Sir, I plan on doing some professional rodeoing."

He nodded and pursed his lips. "Your father says you're the best he's seen."

The best he'd seen? As far as I knew, he'd hardly looked at me for seven years.

"That is true." Denny nodded his head. "He *is* the best my dad has seed. The best for me, too."

I realized my mouth had dropped open, and I quickly closed it. "You've talked to him recently?"

Doc Sidder gave me a smile that made it hard not to look away, but I held my gaze steady. I stood up slowly from the straight chair I'd been sitting in, and I stepped to the wall, leaned one shoulder against it casually.

"I have," he said. "He called last month to set up a place for you to stay before the rodeo." He paused, lowering his head and examining me over the tops of his glasses. "Then he telephoned a few days ago and said you wouldn't be coming after all."

He fell silent, turned his attention to Denny's hand. He pushed around on the swollen parts; Denny shifted his weight from leg to leg and cleared his throat.

I could not stop myself. "Has he called since then?"

"Yesterday."

"Yowch!" Denny's face had gone white, and tears welled in his wide eyes. He tried to snatch his hand away, but Doc Sidder had an iron grip on that, too.

17

"I ALMOST THROWED UP, Will. When the Doc Sidder cut open that snakebite. What comed out was very bad. And the smell. I am glad he wrapped that hand up tight."

I pulled the bed sheet up to Denny's waist. Doc Sidder had said he shouldn't be camping; he wanted to keep a close eye on the wound for a day or two. He asked that I stay too. I told him I'd be back in the morning before the rodeo.

"These sheets are white. On this bed. I am in the white bed. With my white hand. In the white house."

"You'll be just fine here tonight, Denny. I'll come by first thing in the morning to see you. How does that sound?"

Denny was silent for a moment.

"You better come early. I have got things to do."

His eyes were lit up.

"What sort of things, Denny?"

He looked at the ceiling.

"Push that doorbell."

Doc Sidder was waiting for me on the front porch when I left Denny.

"Your father will be here by midday tomorrow, son. He's anxious to talk to you."

What he was anxious for was to get me home looking after Denny again.

"I don't know that there's much to be said."

Crickets were chirping from the bushes on either side of the porch; a car horn beeped down the block; a hot breeze lifted my hair.

Doc Sidder reached out and laid his warm hand on my shoulder. His fingers were long and slender like a piano player's.

"Willard, I'd like you to tell me the truth. Does your father know your plans, or are you running away, son?"

I felt my muscles tighten under his hand, and I took

a step back. If Denny had been out there I would've told him that was a perfect example of an adult not realizing when a boy had grown into a man. I looked up dead into his eyes. My jaw was tight when I spoke.

"I have made some decisions about my future. One of those decisions is to leave the ranch."

"What about Dennis?"

"He followed me. I couldn't get him to go home; he'll go back with my father. He belongs on the ranch."

"Won't you be working a hardship on your father by leaving, Willard? You're of an age now where you must be running some of the operations for him. He must depend on you for a great many things."

I was embarrassed at the choking noise that forced its way up my throat and out into the night air.

"He depends on me to keep Denny out of his hair so he can run things. He depends on me to make sure Denny doesn't walk off a cliff, make sure he gets his chores done, has his shirt buttoned the right way; he depends on me to make sure Denny eats right." I paused for a breath, and a new bucketful of embarrassment splashed over me because of what I'd just said. But I squared my shoulders and added, "I'd appreciate it if you wouldn't call me Willard, sir."

Doc Sidder stuck his hands deep into the front pockets of his trousers. His right hand jingled the coins in there.

"I apologize, Will. For calling you Willard and for assuming I knew what your situation was."

He was silent for a moment as he chinkled the coins and gazed out across the street where all the little houses set even and straight.

"I told you I've known your father a good many years. I had my medical practice in Trinidad when we first met; I removed his appendix and stitched up his head once. I spent time doctoring in the hospital where you and Dennis were born, too. Your father came to see me the day you arrived, to tell me about the birth and about your brother's condition. He asked me what I thought he should do about Dennis. I told him I thought your brother should be institutionalized, put away."

Institutionalized? I felt surprise sweep down my back and through my legs. I had heard of places where they kept the feebleminded, but I had never thought of babies being put there. Never thought of people quitting their own children. I had never thought of Momma or my father weighing a decision like that. . . . I had never thought of Denny locked away from his home, from his family.

"I wonder if things would have turned out differently if your father had followed my advice back then. How old are you boys, Will?"

"Fifteen. Almost sixteen."

"Sixteen years ago." Doc Sidder shook his head. "It's still the most common thing. Most of these children live short lives. Lots of physical problems; their hearts are defective more often than not and give out early. Harder on everyone if they're living in the home. A lot of them, if they make it to Dennis's age, can't even talk."

Over the tops of his eyeglasses his gaze was intense. "You must have devoted a lot of time to him, Will. His speech is quite clear and his ability to follow a conversation, very good. He's reached a level most medical experts don't believe is possible for someone with this deficiency. You have a lot to be proud of. Do you mind my asking how you did it?"

"Well, I . . ." I couldn't think what to say. No one had ever said anything like that to me before. No one had ever said I did something right for Denny, that I taught him important things. No one ever said I must have "devoted a lot" to him. I felt suddenly like I was standing outside myself, looking at a stranger, like I was seeing myself in a photograph for the first time and thinking, "That's not how I pictured myself, that's not what I thought I looked like at all."

"Will?"

I looked up at Doc Sidder. I shrugged. "He's my brother."

18

NO MATTER HOW MANY rocks I pulled out from under my bedroll and tossed away, another one poked me in the back, or the shoulder, or the hip and kept me awake. I threw off the top blanket and let the breeze blow over my bare chest.

I turned onto my belly, propped my elbows up and rested my chin in my hands. I looked into the northwest sky for the Big Dipper and held my arm out straight toward its bright stars, my thumb and pinkie spread wide and my three middle fingers bent to my palm. I stuck my thumb on the star at the top edge of the dipper, furthest from the stem. Just beyond the reach of my little finger was Polaris, the North Star.

My mother taught me how to locate Polaris. "As long as you can find the North Star you can find your way through life. Your grandfather looked up at that same star and your grandfather's grandfather. Keep an eye on it; it can steady you when life makes you shaky."

I rolled onto my side; I needed to sleep. Tomorrow my future would begin; tomorrow I would become a professional cowboy, and I'd need my wits about me and a full head of steam for the rodeo. The rodeo. It was the first time in my seventy-mile journey that I'd had even a moment to consider it. My heart started to beat fast, and my palms were suddenly moist.

I had planned to use my travel time keeping my cowboying skills sharp. I didn't get any practice roping stray junipers, or putting Deep through his paces.

A flash of anger heated my chest. Instead of looking out for my interests, I had looked out for Denny's, as usual. Tomorrow I would compete against riders and ropers better than any I'd ever gone against at home, and unlike me, they'd probably spent the last two days getting ready.

I flipped onto my back, stretched my arms; suddenly, I remembered my rodeo shirt. It was still wadded up in my saddlebag with Denny's vomit on it. I pulled on my pants and boots and rummaged through my things. My hand closed on the cool cotton and the smooth snaps. With the shirt clenched tight in my hands, I knelt on the creek bank and scrubbed the shirt hard in the cold, running water. I pushed it under the surface over and over again and held it there. I pinned it tight to the streambed until no more bubbles rose from it. Until the stench of Denny's vomit was gone. Until Denny was gone from it.

I took a deep breath, and it came easy and soft like a cooling breeze.

I'm going to win, I thought, and a smile settled on my lips. I undressed and slipped back into my bedroll.

I was asleep, and I was in the dream. Denny and I had ridden a long ways out onto the plain. It was gray twilight; the clouds were thick and hid the mesa. I couldn't make out anything familiar in the landscape.

I reined in and turned to tell Denny to take care he didn't yank on the reins when he got off Scooty.

But Denny was already standing on the ground, and

he was talking to our father. They both had their backs to me, so I called out. But the wind was blowing so strong they didn't hear, or they pretended not to.

I walked toward them, calling, but they wouldn't turn around. Finally, I was right behind them, and I tapped both my father and Denny on the shoulder. They still didn't turn, so I walked in front of them.

Right off, I noticed Denny had changed. He looked just like me, and the familiar joy swept through me. Everything had been set right, finally—Denny was who he was supposed to be; we could be real brothers now.

"Denny!"

"Quiet," and he said it in a hard voice. "We're deciding what to do."

"About what?" Fear crept over me.

"Your future," my father said, and they both turned to look at me.

I didn't want to meet their eyes because of what I would see, but I couldn't help myself. I looked into my father's eyes first, and just as I knew it would be, I saw myself reflected there, and I had changed. My mouth hung open, my eyes slanted up.

I looked at Denny; my reflection was the same in his blue eyes.

"You stay here," he said. "It's where you belong."

They got on their horses; they turned and rode away, and I was alone in the gray twilight.

19

"GOOD MORNING, WILLARD." Denny stared at my shirt from the open screen door of Doc Sidder's house. He didn't look me in the eye; he was trying to hurt me. "I see that rodeo shirt is cleaned all up. It looks fancy, Willard."

"How's your hand feel today?"

"I broomed the Doc Sidder's porch with it, Willard."

"I'll change the bandage here pretty quick." Doc Sidder had stepped up beside Denny. He waved me inside. "Would you like some breakfast, Will?"

"Thanks, I already ate." I looked down at the floor. "Have you heard from my father again?"

"Not yet. But, Will, when I do, I'm not going to lie to him about where you are or what Dennis has been through. It's your responsibility to tell him the truth; you owe him that much."

"Yes, sir. I know." I would face up to my father, but I would keep a safe distance, too. I didn't want to get lassoed into returning to the ranch. I was free; I wouldn't ever get roped again. Never.

We followed Doc Sidder through the living room and kitchen and down the two steps to his examination room.

"Come on over here, Dennis, and let's see what we've got. It's time for another dose of sulfanilamide, too."

I felt my whole body swell with relief when I saw Denny's hand. It was still draining, but the bases of his fingers were not puffy anymore, and the red lines had already faded a lot. Doc Sidder washed the bite out again, and Denny winced, but he didn't holler like he had the day before. Doc Sidder powdered the wound and wrapped a clean pad and fresh gauze around it. Denny got his pills down without choking.

The doctor peered at me over his eyeglasses. "You headed out to the rodeo grounds now, Will?"

"Yes, sir."

"Know how to get there?"

"They're out east of town."

"Ride straight down this road; it dead-ends at the entrance. Ten or twelve blocks is all."

"Thanks."

Doc Sidder looked at Denny. "I want you to stay quiet today. Lie down and rest awhile. All right?"

"All right."

"I've got some work to do back here. You boys can talk on the front porch, if you like. Good luck today, Will." Doc Sidder shook my hand.

Denny followed me out, his boots scuffing across the wood planks of the porch. The screen door banged shut behind him.

"Listen, Denny, I have to get going. There's only about an hour until the first event, and I have to get registered and everything."

"All right."

"Well, I just don't know if we'll have much of a chance to talk or say good-bye later, once Father arrives."

"Yeah."

I shrugged. "Well, okay. Take care of yourself. I'll

write, like I promised, and I'll be home to visit, Denny."

I stepped forward and put my arms around him.

His arms hung at his sides.

I dropped mine slowly, and then I turned and walked away.

20

THE SMELL OF HOT POPCORN, finely brushed horses, and fresh manure tickled my nose and made the hairs on the back of my neck stand up. I was in a brand-new world, one where I was not a nursemaid, but a man. A world where I was free. Excitement shot down my spine in a hot tingle.

Yes sir, I was free of my past, free of my brother, and this time I knew for certain that Denny would not follow me. He didn't need to; he was well cared for and well guarded. Denny would end up back where he belonged, and I would end up leading my own life instead of his.

Deep and I rode through crowds of people and cars and horse trailers and concession stands; anticipation swept through me. Everything was loud and fast, and I let myself be carried along, the only thought in my head was of winning all my events and being named the Overall Winner too. The first-place purse would be mine. I had the best horse ever under me, ready to work, and I had my eyes and my hands and my feel for stock and ropes, and my timing. Two days with no practice was nothing. I'd been doing this all my life; I was going to win.

Deep felt everything I felt, and he pranced along, his knees high and each of his ears turning a different direction. The first thing we needed to do was register, and after that I had to find a hazer to partner up with for bulldogging.

Sitting up on Deep, I got a good view of how the place was laid out, and it was easy to spot the line of men standing before the long metal tables; we picked our way through the crowd toward them.

I'd be signing up for bulldogging, calf roping, bucking loose rope horses, and bull riding. That was the order the events would be run in, too. From the safest to the most dangerous. That way most of the cowboys would still be in one piece for the last event, so there would be a big purse and they wouldn't lose the crowd.

I tied Deep to one of the temporary fence sections that had been set up, and I got into line behind a hard-looking cowboy with a cigarette hanging from his lips.

The bald-headed man seated behind the table asked him which events he wanted to sign up for. First thing the cowboy said was "bulldogging."

"Excuse me," I said. "I'm looking for a hazer, and I'd be happy to return the favor."

The cowboy turned around slow and looked way, way down at me, took me in from head to toe. He pulled the cigarette from his mouth, dropped it, crushed it. One side of his mouth smiled at my boots.

"It's a nursemaid you need," he said, and then he turned back to the bald man. He signed up for calf roping, loose rope horse, and bull riding, and picked up his number, 52. Then he turned and walked by me, bumping my shoulder as he passed so I had to take a step back. He didn't say a word.

I kept my head bent low over the registration forms so the burn I still felt in my face wouldn't show. I put down my three bucks for bulldogging; five for my best event, roping; five for loose rope horse; and ten for my second-best event, bull riding. When I turned and walked away with my number, 53, I didn't look left or right.

Me and Deep worked our way around the back of the grounds to where the stock pens were set up. The calves and bulls and broncs were being herded into separate corrals, and none of them was pleased; there was a good deal of bellowing and bawling going on.

My eyes scanned the holding pen in front of me; all the bulls were crowded together, all looking alike until my gaze ran into a wall of red and brown hide that went way up and way sideways. I gave a low whistle.

"You'd need a ladder to get on him," I murmured to Deep.

"Big, ain't he?"

An older man, around fifty maybe, with a drooping salt-and-pepper mustache had pulled up next to me on a chestnut mare.

I gave a nod. I was not anxious to talk to anyone else.

"I heard you say you need a hazer."

Anger started to churn up inside me; I braced for another joke at my expense, my right hand balled into a fist. I wouldn't let this one pass.

"I'll do it." He stuck his right hand out across his horse. "Name's Tim Nater. Folks call me Tater, though. I'm down from Pueblo, from the Lurette Ranch."

I uncurled my hand and reached to shake his.

"Will Bennon, Bennon Cattle Company. Thanks for the offer; I'll take you up on it. Be happy to help you out too."

"I'm mostly just spectating today, but thanks anyway." He turned his horse. "I'll let the registration boys know I'm working with you, and I'll see you over at the arena."

"Thanks again."

I wondered if he was any good. Why would a cowboy miss a day's pay just to watch other people win money? I wasn't going to ask anyone else, though, and the bulldogging purse wouldn't be worth much anyway. If he turned out to be lousy, I wouldn't miss out on but a fraction of what a first-place bull ride would get me.

I turned back to the red giant in the center of the holding pen. Just sitting with your legs spread that wide would tear a groin muscle. I watched how he pushed his way through the other bulls and used his horns on the ones that didn't move quick enough for him; belligerent is what he was. Whoever drew him for a ride would be in for it.

In the next pen over they had the loose rope horses. There were some rough-looking animals, snorting and already bucking. My back started to ache just looking at them. There was an Appaloosa in the bunch, the first one I'd ever seen outside of pictures. Her black mane and spotted blanket made her look wilder than the others, beautiful and untamable. As I stood there watching her, something deep inside of me let go, and I relaxed in a way I hadn't been able to for days.

At last, I was on my own. What I had planned for and worked toward for a year had finally arrived. *I* had finally arrived. No matter how many low-down, ignorant cowpunchers popped up to insult me, I'd just ride right over them and keep going.

A man's voice crackled over the loudspeaker and told all the contestants to make sure they were registered and had their entry numbers pinned on their backs. *First event will be bulldogging*, he said. *All entrants to the west side of the arena.*

It was time.

***

Deep and I blew out the gate at a dead run. The white, mottled steer ahead of us was driving down the center of the arena, but we were already even with his left flank and angling in to him by the time the announcer drawled out my name. From the corner of my eye I saw Tater spur his horse hard: our speed surprised him. He was good, though, that's for sure. Tater got his horse to our pace in a split second and was a perfect mirror of the angle we were setting; the horses formed a tight arrow at the steer's head so he had to slow up hard.

I reached down low over Deep's right shoulder, and a flood of adrenaline rushed through me as my left hand closed around the steer's left horn. I kept stretching out of the saddle until my right hand closed tight on the other horn, and then I swung down off Deep onto the ground, throwing all my weight backward.

From the corner of my eye I saw Tater ride off to the side, his job done.

I locked my spine straight as a board, pointed my toes skyward, and dug my boot heels into the soft dirt. All I could see was thick dust spraying up on either side of us like the Red Sea parting, but I could feel the steer slowing, so I let go my hold on his right horn, sliding my arm around it till I got it wedged tight between my biceps and my forearm.

I focused on his front legs; I wanted to get him stopped while they were coming together, if I could. If he got the chance to splay out and lock them, I'd never get him down.

I got him stopped, and he was not dug in when I started twisting my right arm up and over to the left and pushed down and under on that left horn.

At first his head didn't budge, and I could almost hear the seconds ticking by on the clock; I felt how tight he had his neck braced.

I kept pushing, pushing, and there went his head, twisting away from me. Then boom! Slick as rain I took that boy down to the ground, and he was lying on his left side, and I was sitting on my pockets. I scrambled to my feet, letting loose his horns at the same moment, and he was off again, shaking his head.

Sixteen seconds flat. It was a good time; we'd see if it held.

21

I CHECKED THAT THE LOOP in the end of my pigging string was the right size to slip over the calf's hoof and then clenched the middle of the three-foot cord between my teeth. My heart was pounding; my bulldogging time had lost to two other cowboys. Number 52, the guy with the cigarette and the insults, even set a new record. But all the entrants were dead serious, and they were all mighty fast. I had to wish for a little bit of plain luck, if I was going to be Overall Winner. A couple contestants would have to scratch along the way, miss their toss in calf roping or fall off a bucking horse, something.

"Next number up in calf roping is fifty-three. That's Will Bennon, folks, from the Bennon Cattle Company out on the Mesa de Maya."

My ears tingled at the words. *The Bennon Cattle Company. Mesa de Maya. Home.* My heart twisted; this would be the only day I'd hear those words after my name. In the future I would only hear the name of another rodeo, or somebody else's ranch.

"Let's wish him luck with his calf today. Good luck, Will Bennon."

I had no more time to think; the calf shot out of the gate, and he was a big boy, maybe 375 pounds. His hide was a soft, dark brown, and there was a big puddle of white in the center of his back, trickling down his front legs. He was so scared, his eyes rolled back in his head, and his spindly legs were a blur of speed.

His nose crossed the mark line, and the cowboy holding the ten-foot rubber band across the U-shaped pen we were in let it go. Deep was right behind that dogie in a flash; my rope cut the air like a spinning machete.

I made my throw, letting the rope slide through my right hand, and as soon as I saw it drop over the calf's head, I reined Deep in hard and bailed off his right side and hit the ground running.

Deep was backing up, pulling the calf to me so I didn't have so far to go. I reached over the calf's thick neck with my left hand, reached over his flank with my right, then lifted and pushed with my knee so he lay down flat on his side on the ground with his back to me.

I slipped the pigging string loop over the front leg on his upside and slid it over his hock, then pulled that leg down to meet the back two and began my wraps. Once around all three legs, twice around, and on the third wrap I slid the end of the cord under the top piece of rope and pulled it into a half hitch.

I jumped to my feet and raised both my hands high above my head to show I was done. My hearing suddenly turned back on after the silence of concentration, and I heard the crowd yell and feet stomp in the bleachers; my time must have been as good as it felt.

"Holy cow! Did you see that, folks? Records are breaking like china here today. Will Bennon, if your calf stays put, your time is twelve and three-quarter seconds. Twelve and three-quarters for the cowboy from the Mesa de Maya. Judge will check the rope now, and we'll have a new first place if the tie holds."

I climbed back on Deep and eased him forward,

taking the pressure of the rope off the calf. We were both still keyed up; Deep jigged in place while I stroked his neck and gulped air. I knew we had just bested ourselves, and it was a slick feeling. I wasn't a bit worried about that half hitch holding, either. First place. I drummed the words on Deep's neck.

The judge walked to the calf and flipped him over on his other side. The cord held. He slipped the rope off the calf's head, and I pulled it in and coiled it up. He undid my wrap and tossed the pigging string back to me, and he tipped his hat to me before he walked back to the sidelines. I couldn't help the smile spreading over my face.

"Well, folks, that is indeed a new record for calf roping here in La Junta. Let's hear it for Will Bennon of the Bennon Cattle Company."

The Bennon Cattle Company.

As Deep and I rode out of the arena, I waved my hat to the crowd and found myself searching for Denny's face among all the others.

I held my lead past eighteen other ropers, including number 52. A lot of cowboys didn't compete in anything besides the roping, and now they were going home empty-handed.

The last roping contestant was causing me some anxiety, though. He was a local, but he was the other guy faster than me in bulldogging.

"Number sixty-one, folks, Jim Wassler, second in bulldogging today, let's give him some encouragement in his roping! Let's hear it, folks."

Wassler's calf busted through the gateway, and as quick as his nose crossed the line, Wassler's horse was out of the pen, and they were on that dogie. Wassler legged the calf instead of flanking him like I did. He picked up the calf's left front leg high enough so the left hind came off the ground too, and then just pushed the calf over. He had the pigging string on and three tight wraps done so fast it was only a blur.

"Great job, number sixty-one. Thirteen and a quarter seconds."

First! I had the purse for calf roping.

I was tight before my ride on the loose rope horse. I had just watched my pal, number 52, get thrown off his bucking horse onto his head. That perked me up and improved my chances considerably for Overall Winner, but Jim Wassler was still pressuring me from behind.

I watched as one of the handlers maneuvered a hooked piece of bailing wire under the black gelding I was going to ride and pulled the cinch around in front of the horse's hindquarters. Nobody with a lick of sense tried to do it by hand. These horses hadn't been gentled at all, and their hooves were the wildest part of them.

The handler hooked the cinch tight, then stretched my bucking rope, which would be my only handhold, around behind the front legs the same way.

"Okay, kid, he's all yours."

Kid. My temper flared, but my better sense told me to concentrate on just getting the job done. These cowpunchers would all see soon enough.

I settled down onto the back of my loose rope horse. He twitched and gave a little buck; I hoped that wasn't all he'd be good for. I slid my left hand, palm up, under my bucking rope near the loop in the end and doubled the rope back over itself so I held two layers. The handler helped me snug it up even tighter around the gelding, and then I circled the rope under my clenched hand and pulled myself as far forward as I could, so my groin was up tight against my hand.

"Go!" I yelled, and the gate swung wide.

But my ride turned out to be a big disappointment. I kept my seat on the bucking horse and beat the eight-second bell with no problem, but the black gelding failed to put on a quality show. He bucked all right, but wouldn't come close to a twist or a spin, no matter how hard I spurred him. The horse got an eighteen and a nineteen score from the judges, and my scores were both low, too—nineteens.

The only consolation was that Jim Wassler didn't have any better luck with his loose rope horse. I felt a good deal better until number 81, Carlos Alvarez, took his ride. Through dumb luck the horse that got crowded into the bucking gate for him was a wild beast. Number 81 was gripping the loose rope in his left hand like it was a life preserver in the middle of the ocean. His right hand was high in the air, and the gray horse under him bucked and jumped and did quarter twists in different directions with his front end and his hind end while all four feet were in the air.

The eight-second bell rang, and Carlos Alvarez swung his right leg over the horse's neck, slid off its left side, and strolled toward the sidelines like he was leaving the lunch counter in a diner. The crowd went nuts, and I couldn't help clapping and whistling too, for his lucky draw and his skill.

Number 81 smiled up at the packed bleachers and lifted his hat.

"Carlos Alvarez, ladies and gentlemen. It's easy to see why he was Overall Winner of the Big Sky Rodeo. Number eighty-one, a real professional. Let's hear it for him, folks."

When the roar died down his scores were announced. "For the rider Carlos Alvarez, number eighty-one, scores of twenty-one and twenty-two. For the horse, Devil Foot, twenty and twenty-one. Fantastic score, eighty-four points, folks, for the cowboy and the bronc. Let them hear how much you liked that ride."

I hadn't heard the times that number 81 racked up for bulldogging or calf roping, but I'd have bet they were more than decent.

Now with the loose rope horse scores I was tied with Jim Wassler for second place, and Carlos Alvarez had the lead.

It had all come down to the most dangerous event of all: bull riding.

22

HANDS WORKED THREE different chutes for the bulls, so as soon as one rider was safely off another could go. I'd be up quick. With care I checked every square inch of my bucking rope. Any tears or weak spots from my loose rope horse ride would make getting on the bull even more dangerous than it had to be.

I was starting to hope that big red bull would be mine to ride. I needed points to get into first and stay there, and Big Red was bound to score high with the judges. Any rider that stayed on him and beat the bell would have to get a perfect score. A perfect score would clinch the Overall Winner title for me. It would clinch it for Alvarez or Wassler, too.

I got myself into line at the number two chute and watched while the men ahead of me took their last chance to win points. As number 39 was called I took a closer look at the bulls. Big Red was still in the holding pen; he had another bull cornered, prodding him with his horns. He was as far away from the gate as a bull could get. The chutes held only two animals each, though, so he could still push his way on up front and be mine.

I watched numbers 48 and 49 ride, and 49 got yanked loose from his bull. He spun through the air and plowed face-first into the dirt. He came up spitting dust and dripping blood. His nose wasn't quite in the middle of his face anymore.

A chill wriggled down my spine, and I wondered if maybe I couldn't get a perfect score from just a regular-size bull. I looked into the holding pen, everywhere in the holding pen. Big Red was not there; he was already in one of the chutes.

Slowly, I turned and looked at chute number two, the one I would ride from. Big Red was there, first in line. Disappointment and relief washed over me. The bull behind him, the one I would ride, looked just fine.

He was big and black, slathering and drooling saliva. Leave Big Red to number 50; I could get the job done on this boy.

They had gotten poor old number 49 and his broken nose out of the arena and chased off the bull that did it to him. "Let's hear another round of applause for Dicky Lee Jost, folks. He'll be thinking of this ride for some time to come. Gave it a good try. Number forty-nine. And now, it's number fifty from gate two. Joshua Lambert from the Cross L Ranch in La Mar. Let's wish him luck, folks. Joshua Lambert."

There was static and bumping from the loudspeaker for a moment, and then the announcer's voice came again. "Correction, folks. Joshua Lambert is a scratch. Number fifty-one will be up next, and that'll be from gate number three. Right now, here comes Dan Bickell, and he looks like he's up to the challenge. Wish him luck."

It took me only a moment to realize what that scratch meant for me: I would be riding Big Red.

"Give me your bucking rope, kid."

I looked up at a tall, lean man with a lazy eye. Silently, I handed my rope to him.

"I don't know if it's long enough, boy, that bull's got such a barrel chest on him."

I saw his straight eye wink at one of the other men; my face heated up.

He threaded the cinch onto the bailing wire and tightened it up in front of Big Red's back legs. He stretched my bucking rope behind the front legs, and, suddenly, it was time for me to climb onto the monster's back.

Hanging over the top rail of the chute I saw just how wide he really was and how rough his hide. It was peppered with digs from horns or fence wire he had punished. Running from one side of his broad neck to the other was a wide, scaly white scar.

I climbed higher and swung over the top rail. I came down so I was just above the bull's back, stretched my left leg as far over him as I was able. A muscle in my hip started to knot up with the stretch, and I realized that must be how Denny felt every time he climbed on Scooty. Slowly, I lowered myself, and before I was even set all the way down, Big Red bellowed and threw himself into the air, slamming into the sideboards trying to get rid of me. I rammed my left hand under my bucking rope and doubled the rope back. The hands helped me snug it up even tighter around Big Red, and I circled the rope under my clenched hand and pulled my groin up tight against my hand. I held on to one of the slats in the gate and gave a hard nod to show I was set.

Big Red crashed sideways into the boards, mushing my leg like a loaf of fresh bread.

"Better get him out quick, Buz, or he'll be done before he starts."

I felt my jaw clench down hard with anger, but it disappeared quick as Buz pulled the gate open from the far side, and I caught the last part of the announcer's sentence, ". . . riding Tiny Tim." I felt like laughing, but I didn't want to bite through my tongue.

Tiny Tim thumped across the dirt arena, kicking up dust, lifting my joints out of their sockets, but I stayed with him. I even gave him a spur on the right, and he began to buck. His front legs lurched off the ground, and I hugged him tight with my legs and leaned forward to counterbalance.

His hind end spiraled up in a quarter twist, but I had a good seat, and as he crashed down on his fore legs, I threw my arm up and behind my shoulder to pull my upper body back so his forward thrust wouldn't throw me off.

He jumped all four feet up and twisted his front half 180 degrees, then slammed the hard ground again. Something in my spine made a crunching noise, but it didn't loosen my grip. The only pain I felt for sure was the inside of my thighs from doing the splits.

Every time I drew a breath I pulled more dust into my throat, and the only thing I could see clearly was that dug-up red neck with the ugly white zigzag across it.

Up came those front legs, and I turned my shoulder into the bull and pushed into him with my left leg as he spun his front end out to the left. I had him good.

His back legs rocketed up, and all of a sudden my timing and balance were off; I was riding back on my pockets. His hooves crashed to the ground, and my pelvis sat far back from my handhold. I tried to jump myself forward, back into position, and just then the bell rang loud and clear, and I knew I'd made it and had my best ride ever.

I went to swing my right leg over him and slide off. I saw the crowd was on its feet, I heard the roar, but as my leg came forward over that wide scar, Tiny Tim threw himself high into the air and slammed down on his front legs.

I saw my body was stretched out way in front of my left hand; my hold ripped loose from the rope and I hurtled forward. I heard the bull snorting; I saw tan-colored, rutted horns come at my face; and then my eyes turned off as blunt, shattering pain cracked through my head and exploded down my spine.

23

I TRIED TO MOVE MY arms, my legs; they wouldn't budge. Cold terror rushed through me as my brain struggled to understand, and I had the notion I'd been bitten by a rattlesnake. The venom had paralyzed me; I'd be dead soon.

I fought to sit up, but I was far too dizzy for that, and my brain told me the floodwaters of the Purgatoire were spinning me around, just like a trout.

A day passed, or maybe a moment. I opened my eyes; the sky was brown and there was chewed gum stuck to it.

I heard a voice far in the distance.

"Oh, Wi-ill. How are you feeling?"

I knew that voice, I was sure of it. "Momma?"

"Hi," it said.

A face floated in front of mine. I thought it was a young face; I groped to call it by name. "Tiny Tim?"

"It is me, Will. It is Denny."

"Huh?"

"The rodeo man told me you were here. You have been asleeping."

My memory lit up in a flash. "My bull ride. How many points did I get, Denny?"

Denny was silent for a moment. "When you ask that then I say: eighty-eight. That's what the rodeo man said."

Eighty-eight points; I closed my eyes again for a minute and savored the news. It wasn't perfect, but was darn near. "Is that first, Denny? Am I the Overall Winner?"

"That rodeo man said first on the bull. But tie for Overall. That is what he said, Will."

I lay perfectly still and didn't speak for a minute, waiting for the dizziness to ease up. "What do I have to do to win?"

"That rodeo man said 'rope-off.' He wants for you to get up now, I think."

Gingerly, I propped myself up on my elbows. My ears started to ring. "Where am I exactly?" I was confused about the chewed gum above my head.

"That rodeo man put you under this table. He said 'for shade.' He is nice, Will."

I turned onto my side and then onto my belly, rested, and finally I rolled into the hot July sunshine. I lay on my back and stared up into the blue sky with no chewed gum stuck to it. The world made sense again.

"Will, you have hurts on your face. You have got a lump right there."

"Ow. Don't poke at me."

"Sorry. I'm sorry, Will. There are rocks stuck in your face." He pointed, but didn't touch me again.

"The top of your face is black, Will."

"How did you get here, Denny?"

"I runned."

I pushed myself onto my hands and knees. My head felt so big from the inside, I had to check it. Slowly, I raised my hands and felt it all around. It seemed regular from the outside.

"Give me a hand up, Denny." He yanked on my arm so hard, my head throbbed.

"You look sick, Will."

"I'm fine. I might have a little concussion. My head feels like the time I fell off the back of the pickup and landed on it."

"Maybe you shouldn't rope-off. You should go under the table again."

"I'll be steady once I'm up on Deep. Where is he?"

Denny pointed to my left. Deep was tied to the fence section right by the registration table I had just crawled out from under.

I concentrated real hard and aimed carefully. My foot slid into the stirrup; I hauled my leg over. I did feel better being in the saddle.

"Which way is the arena, Denny?" Everything looked the same to me, all the pens and the gates.

Denny turned around twice. "Maybe there." He pointed over to the low, whitewashed concrete walls. I could see the bleachers.

"All right, I'm going."

Denny was blurry around the edges, but I could see his mouth twisted to the side and the little shake of his head before I turned Deep and walked away.

I zeroed in on the wall, and when I got to it, I followed

its curve until I came to the holding pen full of calves.

The three hands looked up as I got close, and they all smiled big and reached up and slapped me on the back when I stopped. My ears started to ring again.

"Can't get enough, huh, kid?"

"That was the best ride I've seen a kid make, even without the wreck."

The third cowboy jogged off toward the announcer's stand.

"I'm not a kid."

"Well, folks," the announcer's voice blared, "Will Bennon is recovered from his run-in with that killer bull, and he says he's ready for the rope-off to break the first-place tie for Overall Winner today!"

The applause that answered the announcement was deafening; it made the roar in my head almost unbearable. I leaned off Deep's left side and retched, wiped my mouth with my sleeve. When I was sure I wouldn't throw up again, I turned to the hands. They were watching me with a mix of disgust and wonder.

"Who am I tied with?"

"Eighty-one. The hotshot that won the Montana rodeo."

The loudspeaker crackled, and the announcer's voice ricocheted in my head. "Will Bennon will be going first. We'll give him just a minute to get fixed up, folks." The voice kept booming while Deep and I were making our way into the U-shaped pen. The cowboy grinned at me while he stretched the rubber band across the opening and held it tight.

"You ready, Ace?" the announcer asked.

Even with my brain swelled, I appreciated the title; I pushed my right hand high into the air to signal that I was.

"All righty, folks. We're in for a treat. This cowboy's been proving himself all day. Show him what you think, won't you?"

The cheers, the clapping, the stomping feet were too much for Deep, and he bounced around so I thought my head would split. I leaned off to the side and retched again, and I saw the calf's hooves shoot past me. I lifted my head in time to see him cross the line, and without a thought, I spurred Deep, and we were on him like professionals.

My rope dropped square over his head. Deep sat back; my stomach lurched, but I was not going to vomit in front of the crowd. I jogged up to the calf, but I couldn't figure out how to start. Something was different. It took me a minute to realize I was in front of him instead of in back.

I felt confident about flanking the calf, and I set about it, but my parts wouldn't cooperate. The calf hopped back on his legs, and I had to wrestle him down again, and then the pigging string loop wouldn't go over his upside leg.

I got my three wraps done, but it looked like four, and my fingers felt fat; they fumbled over each other, and I couldn't get the rope going the right way for the half hitch.

Finally, I tottered to my feet and looked around. I remembered I needed to raise my arms; it was so hard to push them up into the air. The roar of the crowd engulfed me, or maybe it was the roar in my head. I looked back at Deep, and I saw him shake his head and look away. Just before everything went black and silent, I realized I had never seen a horse do that before.

24

I WAS IN A DARKENED ROOM. There was no chewing gum on the ceiling, and nothing was spinning. The roar in my head was gone, and my ears were not ringing. My head ached, but my thoughts were clear. My spine felt knotted up, and my right leg felt shorter than my left, but I could move them both. I wondered where I'd been and where I was, and an image of my hands and my pigging string popped into my mind. The memory of the whole rope-off swept in and crushed me so flat so quick I couldn't breathe. I had not won; I'd made a fool of myself standing there gawking at the calf like I'd never seen one before.

But then memories of the rest of the rodeo came, and relief and new hope washed over me. My calf roping time was the best and there was my ride on Tiny Tim, my 88 points. "Ace," the announcer called me. Even without the Overall Winner's purse, I bested most of the other cowboys.

I'd go back to the rodeo grounds, wherever they were. I'd collect my prize money and talk to the stock handlers like I planned. I started to push myself up to sit, but my stomach rolled, and my head spun and pounded like I was back on the bull. I couldn't hold myself up; I couldn't get back to the rodeo. I floated down and down. I heard a moan when my head settled on the pillow.

Anger started to well inside me, pushing and bouncing against the pain so I thought I'd explode.

Who had brought me here? Who took me away from the rodeo before I could land a job?

Who whisked me away from my future so I couldn't claim it?

"Hi. Hi, Will. Glad to see you."

Slowly I turned my head toward Denny. He was leaning over the bed; his slanted blue eyes were dancing, and he was wearing a wide jack-o'-lantern grin. Suddenly I felt like I was in the dream, and I was so glad the room was too dark for me to see my reflection in his eyes.

"Will! I have a surprise to tell. I have got a plan. I am a grown-up now too. Because of my own plan. I am going to stay here. At the Doc Sidder's. For a while. Our dad and the Doc Sidder have talked it over. Then they askded me. I had to say 'okay.' No one else could say it. So I said it. Now I am going to do the things like at home. Chores. Like at home when I reach under the chickens for their eggs. When I put them in the blue basket. And I am going to sweep the broom for the Doc Sidder. I am going to wash dishes. And some forks and knifes. And something new. I am going to fold the Doc Sidder's towels. For his sick people. He says he can teach me that. He says I can learn it. So, I am a grown-up. Like you, Will." Denny paused. "What is the problem, Will? Are you hurting? Does your lump hurt you?"

I forced my face muscles to relax so my brain would quit surging against my skull, but I could not stop the hot tears that prickled over my cheeks. I could not stop the tears.

25

I DIDN'T KNOW HOW MUCH time had passed when I opened my eyes again and saw not Denny leaning over me, but my father. His face was thawed by the warm light of the bedside lamp.

In his eyes was a look I knew from long ago; it made me want to turn away. I recognized it, but I couldn't think why or from when exactly.

"Will," he said. "Son."

A tight braid of surprise and embarrassment twisted through me hearing his voice shake.

He cleared his throat.

"Malcolm—Dr. Sidder—says you'll be fine; you've got a concussion, and you're low on fluids, that's all."

The bedsprings squeaked as my father stood up. His

boot heels tapped the floorboards; his shadow stepped back from the bed.

"I picked up your winnings for you. You took the purse for roping and bull riding. Hundred fifty-five dollars for roping, Will. One-eighty for bull riding. That's a year's salary working for me."

I was surprised again; his voice was full of pride.

My father's boots scuffed the floor as his shadow shifted its position on the wall.

"The foreman from the Lurette Ranch up in Pueblo wants to hire you on. Fellow named Nater. Said he was hazer for you in the bulldogging."

A gasp escaped me; I hoped my father didn't hear it.

My heart raced.

My future! I had my future after all.

I proved myself.

I won my freedom.

I was on my way.

"Will."

My father's voice startled me.

"I want you to come home with me."

26

I COULD NOT SLEEP. My father had left me hours before so I could rest, but my skull felt several sizes too small for my brain, and my back and neck had tightened up enough that any little movement made me catch my breath.

Every once in a while I heard a car go past, and its shadow drove across the bedroom wall. The sight made me uncomfortable deep inside; it made my heart ache for the silhouettes of coyotes and hootie owls.

My mind would not let go of the image of my father's eyes. I knew why I recognized the look in them. It was from seven years ago, and it went with the words, "Your mother loves you from Heaven now." The pain I saw in his eyes then, and the pain I'd seen earlier was the same. I didn't know if I could turn my back on it.

My father said he needed my help on the ranch.

As bad as it hurt to move, my thoughts wouldn't let me lie still. I dragged myself up to sit, and I couldn't tell if the groan I heard came from me or the bed. My muscles were in knots, and my heart was too. I didn't have the strength to keep my longing for home pushed down anymore. It had grown and swelled ever since my father asked me to go back with him.

Ever since he told me of the Pueblo offer.

Ever since I realized I was on the edge of stepping off into the future I'd been dreaming of and riding toward.

My father told me things would be different if I went back home with him. "You're a man, Will. It's time you took your rightful place." He said if I wasn't satisfied with the new arrangements there, with things changed, I wouldn't have to stay.

My father told me I could leave the ranch if I wanted to. And he told Denny he could come back to it. A sigh from deep inside me sent a hot streak of pain from the back of my head all the way to my toes.

27

EARLY THE NEXT MORNING, the truck idled on the street before Doc Sidder's place; my father was already behind the wheel waiting on me.

"Will." Doc Sidder shook my hand and held on to it for a moment. "It was a pleasure to meet you. I wish you good luck, son. Be certain to take it easy for another couple days. I know you're improved over yesterday, but it takes more than a night to mend a concussion and get the fluids back into you."

"I will. Thank you, sir. Thanks for fixing me up, and Denny."

Denny stuck his hand out to me then, and we shook. He stepped forward and wrapped his arms around me gently. "I wish you luck too, Will. And bemember, we are brothers. Blood brothers."

He nodded hard to make sure I agreed.

"Brothers is something you don't forget," he said. "Even when we are gone from each other."

I tried to smile. "I'll remember."

I checked that Scooty and Deep were locked into the horse trailer good and tight, and then climbed into the passenger's side of the pickup. Father shifted into first gear, and slowly we pulled away.

I looked in the sideview mirror. Denny was standing there. He lifted onto his toes, raised his arms high, and made a cross with his index fingers. My hands flew up, echoing his, and then the pickup turned the corner, and we were both lost from view.

The snaking black road went on forever. I dozed off and on, and every time I woke up I felt fine for a second, and then my head would start to pound and my stomach jumped as I realized where I was, and where I was going.

I looked over at my father. His eyes stayed on the road. As I watched him, I thought of what Doc Sidder told me about Father having to decide whether to keep

Denny with the family. I tried to picture what he looked like then; he would've been, let's see, thirty-five or so, I guess, younger, darker-haired, straighter in the back. Suddenly I remembered his smile, the one he had when Denny and I were small. It lit up his whole face . . . and my heart. It had been years since I'd seen it. All he managed anymore was a weary stretch of his lips.

"Why did you decide to keep Denny?"

The question jumped out loud and strong and ricocheted back and forth between us. I dropped my head down quickly so I couldn't see if his face changed, but from the corner of my eye I saw him turn to me.

He was silent. I knew he heard me, but it was his decision whether to answer or not.

"I believed you were Denny's only hope for having any kind of life. I thought you would help him develop as much as he could."

"What does that mean?"

"You're brothers. You're twin brothers. The same blood runs through your veins. I believed you would love Denny in a way no one else would. I believed you would walk alongside of him, protect him, teach him. And you did. I never regretted the decision."

He never regretted the decision. Anger welled up inside of me. It gushed up my throat and pushed a quick, harsh breath out of my mouth. There were thoughts and feelings and words rising like sulfur steam in a geyser; for the first time I understood that Denny was not the problem. Denny was never the problem. It wasn't Denny who made the decisions of my life for me, it was my father. He had decided what my life would be a long time before, when I was only a couple days old.

"What about me? What about *my* life, the hope for *my* life? Who did you think would teach me the things *I* needed to know?" It was all out in the air now, spinning like a twister, threatening both of us.

His answer stopped me cold; his answer sucked all the air out of the truck cab. His answer was a single word.

"Denny," he said.

28

DENNY? I SAT STOCK-STILL; a numbness stole through my bones, turning them brittle. Denny's name tapped itself out over and over inside my head like a telegraph message. Denny. What had *he* ever taught me? How to live with a heartache so big and so hungry it always threatened to swallow me whole? How to live with my insides scorched by anger hotter, more dangerous than lightning? Denny.

When I finally let the question escape into the air, it was only a hiss.

"What did Denny ever teach me?"

My father's jaw tightened. He was silent for a long moment, and then let out a deep breath.

"Not the outside things, Will. Not reading or writing, not riding, or roping."

He glanced over at me; the pain was back in his eyes.

"I've seen Denny interrupt you a million times when you were working at something you wanted to do, something you cared about. And the same million times I've seen you set your task aside and listen to your brother, or help your brother, or remind him what to do. You learned tolerance from Denny, Will. And you learned patience. How old was he before he ended up with his right boot on his right foot more than half the time? He finally got it down because you had patience with him. And he's the one that taught it to you. You learned a hell of a lot from him about what it means to truly care for another human being . . . and you learned a lot more about being a man than I ever knew."

My eyes jumped off the road and met his, and I didn't even care that he'd see them watering up because his were, too.

"I made mistakes, Will. When your mother died I told myself I wanted you and Denny to stay close, so I buried myself in work on the ranch and left you to be mother and father to Denny instead of his brother. It wasn't fair, it wasn't right, and what I finally confessed to myself is that it wasn't only to keep you two close that I turned my back. Just as much, I wanted to stop feeling, quit feeling anything. Your mother's death broke me, took the balance out of the world."

I braced my hands on my knees and spoke low so my voice would be steady.

"It was like you both died that day. Like I lost both of you."

My father turned away for a minute, looked out the side window, but I saw his shoulders shake.

"I can't change anything in the past, Will, only the future."

29

AS THE PICKUP SWUNG past the barn, I saw Hank's head pop up from behind his truck. He was tossing a roll of fencing into the back. He gave a wave, and a big smile broke over his face. My smile matched his.

The telephone was ringing when we stepped into the house. My father answered it and was silent for several minutes.

"That's fine, Denny," he said. "I'm glad to hear it. Yep, I'll put him on."

He handed the telephone to me, and his lips stretched again. "Malcolm told him he could call."

"Denny?" I said.

"Hi. Hi, Will. How are things there? At home."

"Everything's good, Denny."

"Did you have a good ride home?"

I was silent, thinking of what I wanted to say.

"Will? I can't see if you are there. Are you there?"

"Denny, I'm proud of you. I'm real proud of you."

"Uh! What? What did I do? Will?"

"A lot, Denny. So much."

Later, after supper, after resting, I grabbed my rifle, saddled up Deep and rode out. The sun was still burning down, but the shadows were stretching out. The air smelled of sage. A gray rabbit hopped behind a rock just to my left.

A feeling nagged at me, that I needed to go home and tell Denny to collect the eggs, and then I remembered. I meant it when I told him I was proud of him. Denny was brave. He was also ambitious. I had been mulling over what my father said about my teaching Denny, about my helping him in ways no one else could, or would. And I had also thought about what my father believed Denny taught me.

These last few days wouldn't have stood as testament to my patience or tolerance; a lot of days in the last fifteen years wouldn't have backed up the claim either.

The old anger was still inside me, and it was very dark and very much alive. Maybe it would always be there. Decisions got made that would last a lifetime.

But it was not the threat it had been before. I wasn't scared it might drag me under, drown me.

There were other feelings swirling around it, feelings that were new to me: admiration for Denny, for what he'd done; and satisfaction, in how much I'd helped him. Father and Doc Sidder were right; he wouldn't have gotten as far as he had without me. The way Denny's and my lives had been wrapped around each other suddenly felt more like an accomplishment than the familiar heartache.

A crow flapped over my head, his ragged, black wing tips pressed against the blue sky. From out at the reservoir I heard cattle lowing. Our cattle.

Another feeling seeped through me, and it took me a minute to realize it was ease.

I had missed this land. What peace I had ever found had been out here in the open spaces of the ranch, in the breeze running through tall grass, in the long hind feet of jackrabbits, and in the bronze leaves of the scrub oak in the fall.

"Will?"

I jumped. Deep didn't move; he'd been watching my father ride up while I was lost in thought.

"Will? There's twenty head down by Calf Pasture Reservoir I'd like to get moved still today. Could you move them?"

I felt my chin drop. "Me? I mean, by myself?"

I saw my father's lips stretch, and I knew they were trying for that old, lost smile. He nodded.

"Hank thinks the pasture by Pacheco's Water Hole is good for a couple weeks. If you agree, leave them there. If not, try the next one west." My father turned his horse. "And, Will, Hank said one of the calves down there had a shade of lameness the other day. I'd like you to check him out too. Let me know what you think."

I nodded and watched my father ride north, back toward the house. When he was only a speck I turned Deep south and urged him into a trot. As we came up over a rise my eye caught the wave of a short, mangy, tan tail before it disappeared behind an outcrop of basalt. It took my mind a minute to register what it was: the coyote I'd been gunning for.

And Denny could not save him this time. I pressed

Deep's sides, and he was into a lope before I could blink; he knew. We angled together around the outcrop, straightened out on the other side. I spotted that durned coyote, and he knew we were onto him. He pumped his back legs for all he was worth, staying low to the ground and making straight for Cobert Canyon. I figured he would run down and then up when the walls of the canyon were too steep for me and Deep.

Bloodlust had me by the throat. I knew it was not just the coyote I wanted to kill, it was a huge, red bull with a zigzag scar, and a river, and it was my brother's pain and my father's, too. It was whoever or whatever decreed that my mother should die.

With my legs I felt Deep's heaving sides; my heart pounded against my ribs and in my head. My ears were ringing again, so that was all I heard, and I did not care, not one bit. I saw a rock coming in our path and I hunkered down; Deep jumped it, and we hummed across the grass, dipping down into Cobert Canyon. We came over another rock on the trail, and I caught sight of the coyote again.

"Go, go, Deep!"

My hands clenched the reins; I was riding low on his

neck. We were so close I could see the coyote's pink tongue hanging out the side of his mouth and blowing back toward us. He was slowing up; we were wearing him down.

I saw he was going to break right toward the canyon wall. I cut Deep hard that direction and drove him forward. Suddenly we were in front of the coyote. My eyes locked onto his, and he stopped, paralyzed. His eyes were yellow, with specks of another color in them, and they had given up. He looked away. His sides heaved, saliva dripped from his tongue, his short, scrawny tail fell to the ground.

My pulse beat in my stomach, my head, in my hands. I brought my rifle out slow and easy. I lifted it to my shoulder, I sited on the coyote, I cocked the gun. I looked into his yellow, flecked eyes.

This time he met my gaze and did not turn away. There was something familiar in his look, something that echoed in my heart and pained me. With a start I recognized it, named it. Resignation. The resignation I had felt my whole life, every time Denny tracked *me* down. Every time he had cornered *me*.

I had the devil square in my sites, the killer I had

been tracking so long, so very long.

I tightened my finger on the trigger.

Sweat dripped from my forehead and ran into my eyes, making them burn.

I lifted the rifle a fraction more, concentrating, and then I pulled the trigger with all my might.

I fired the shot high over the canyon wall, into the darkening sky.

The coyote flinched, but still holding my eye, he tilted his scruffy tan muzzle up toward the rising star Polaris. His voice filled the sweet air with a short, triumphant howl, and then he was gone.

Alive.

Free.

Like me.

Like Denny. My brother Denny.

EXTRAS

A SMALL WHITE SCAR

Meet K. A. Nuzum

I am a child of the wild, wild eastern plains of Colorado, where the winds howl long and lonely in the winter and the sun bakes the land hard and dry in the summer, and you can still find cowboys riding horses and herding dusty cows.

Cowboys and horses were always a big part of my life. When I was a kid there were *lots* of them on TV; *Rawhide* and *Gunsmoke* were the biggest hits of the day, and they featured handsome, hard-working cowboys and handsome, hard-working horses.

My weekly allowance went toward renting horses to ride for two hours at a stretch at the stable east of town, and weekend afternoons found me loping my rented steed across flat, open meadows.

Even greater than my fondness for cowpokes and horses was my love for writing. I have known since third grade that I wanted to be a writer. My first piece of fiction, *The Adventures of Super Star*, was penned, along with other early "masterpieces," at our town's bowling alley. On Thursday evenings my friend and I accompanied her parents to their league play, and while the grown-ups bowled, we wrote our first stories.

Funny, though I so loved cowboys and horses, I didn't spend much time reading about them. When I read, which I did a *lot*, my favorites were Edward Eager's magic books, Jean George's *My Side of the Mountain*, anything about King Arthur, and first above all others, the Time-Life book on dinosaurs. Oh, yeah.

I didn't end up settling down with a cowboy, but I do have three horses, along with five dogs, three cats, one pot-bellied pig, one chicken, one roofing contractor husband, and two large sons . . . and I'm still writing.

Behind the Scenes

The landscape of *A Small White Scar* plays an integral part in your story and is as much a character as your actual characters. Why were you inspired to write about the great outdoors?

It's pretty tough to write a Western and not have the landscape play a large part in the story. The land is part of our whole cowboy myth; nature is the eternal, unyielding adversary that the cowboy or pioneer or explorer must always grapple with and either be beaten by or make peace with. The land is what builds strength and character in a man or a woman.

I was first introduced to the landscape of *A Small White Scar* nearly twenty-five years ago. When I first visited my friend's ranch, which begins in the shadow of the Mesa de Maya and spreads south from there, I honestly felt like I'd found home. I stood in the middle of seemingly endless grasslands turned pink and bronze by the bright days and chill nights of autumn. My socks and sneakers were sheathed in cockleburs I'd shuffled through, my cheeks were numbed by the rising wind of the late afternoon, and my heart as well as my eyes were filled by the vast, harsh beauty of the place. The ranch is *so* big you can't help but feel teeny when you're on it. It isn't a smallness that makes you feel lost or diminished at all; rather, it's exhilarating, liberating. It is a smallness that you inhale as the scent of sage and absorb into your blood, your brain, your heart,

your soul. It's a smallness that comes from the powerful realization that you belong to the world.

You don't stand outside of it, you don't control it, you are part of it, a thread in its rich tapestry. *That* is a landscape worth writing about.

"Brothers is something you don't forget," Denny says to his twin brother, Will. The relationship these brothers have is so genuine and true. Are Will and Denny based on real people?

Uh-uh, Will and Denny aren't specific individuals. They are more an amalgam of people I have known, relationships I have had or have had a bird's eye view of.

Will and Denny each have a small white scar on their left index fingers, an indelible mark of the many bonds they share. Did you ever make such a mark with your sister or a friend when you were younger? What did it signify?

I had a few blood sisters when I was a kid. The pacts were usually made when one of us got a scrape and was already bleeding, and we used it as an opportunity to swear eternal allegiance to each other. I don't think we ever used enough blood, though; the promises were quickly forgotten.

Will and his horse, Deep, are partners, compañeros, "about as close as a two-legged fifteen-year-old and a four-legged eight-year-old could be." Did you have a horse or other pet that was your Deep?

Deep is based very much on my quarterhorse Dan. Someday I will write a book just about him. How he came to be ours is quite a tale, and the story of the serious injury he got during a hail and lightning storm just three weeks after he came to us is pretty dramatic, too. He is one of the best and most precious surprises of my life. Dan is so beautiful, he's all white with a dark mane and tail, he's got big ol' mule ears, and golden eyes like a goat. He is incredible to ride; his gaits are all really, really smooth because he has just a bit of Fox Trotter in his bloodline. He is also smart. Too smart. He's an escape artist; if you leave the barn door unlocked even for a second, Dan bumps it open with his nose and either gets into the grain barrel right away, if he has time, or, if you're hot on his trail, he trots out through the barn lickety-split to the back pasture to snag a few mouthfuls of long grass before you nab him. Every ounce of love and respect Will feels for Deep, I feel for Dan.

Quick Questions

1. What does "K. A." stand for?
K. A. stands for Kathleen Ann. I think it was a law during the middle of the 1950s that all girls had to have Ann for their middle name.

2. Western or English (saddle, that is)?
WESTERN!

3. What's your favorite event to watch in the rodeo?
Bull riding.

4. Did you ever participate in a rodeo?
Only neighborhood ones with bicycles.

5. Have you ever come face-to-face with a rattlesnake?
Accidentally at summer camp. I backed away nice and slow, pard.

6. Have you ever eaten rattlesnake steak?
Yup. Yuck. It wasn't out on the open range, though; it was in a fancy restaurant. It's amazing how much you can charge to serve people snake for dinner.

An Excerpt from
K. A. Nuzum's New Book,

The Leanin' Dog

5

A Lump of Brown

NEVER BEFORE HAD one of my daymares come ascratching. My knees started to knock again as I crossed to the door. I pressed my ear to its rough wood, listening.

The scratching came. And a soft whine. From down low.

I circled my fingers around the door latch and closed them tight. I didn't feel like I was being taken by a daymare; I didn't feel like I was slipping away. I felt the cold latch in my fingers and the cold air coming in under the door. I heard the scratching and the whining.

I tugged my woolen cap down one-handed and pulled my stubbornness up from deep inside, and I lifted the latch and pushed the door. . . . It didn't budge.

"Mayhap it was the wind after all; mayhap the wind caused the snow to drift and pile up against the cabin door," I said.

The idea swelled my courage, and I drew back and then butted my shoulder hard against the door. Cold air swiped at my cheeks as the door jumped open a crack, but right away it slammed shut again.

"We'll see about that," I said, and it was through clenched teeth. I backed up to the table and pushed off it to give me a powerful start, and I heaved my whole self square at the door. It swung wide, and I went with it, barreling into the great outdoors.

As my hands flew to my ears, my eyes flew to the big, snow-covered lump of brown that was struggling to its feet smack dab in front of me. I tried to sidestep it, but my feet were going too fast, and the stoop was slick, and so I ran full into the lump and fell square on top of it.

I let out a grunt when I landed, and the lump yelped and squirmed and wriggled out from under me. It took off lickety-split toward the woods.

I pushed myself onto my knees and peered through

the curtain of snow.

Why, it was a dog! Not a daymare at all, but a dog had come ascratching at the door. Something was wrong with one of its legs, though. There were four of them, but the right front one acted like it belonged to someone else. It swung wide of the body instead of underneath it, as if it was trying to get away on its own.

"Here, dog," I called. "Come back!"

The dog stopped, and I filled with hope when she turned around. She looked at me, cocking her head.

"Oh, please, won't you come back?" I called to her. "Come back and keep me company?"

The dog stood for a long minute, sizing me up, and I drank in the sight of her.

Fudge-brown was the color of her coat, and the white snow piled up in a broad stripe down her back from her ears to her wagging tail. She was so big, her head was wide and square, and her flopped-over ears were a deeper brown than her body. She had them pricked, listening to me, and they looked like they were straining to stand up all the way. Her tail was long and feathered along its bottom edge. She was beautiful.

As I watched, the dog tilted her muzzle high, and across the distance I heard what she'd said.

"Roo!"

And then she loped away from me, into the woods, that right front leg trying to go north while the rest of her headed west.

"No! Wait, oh please, wait."

I scrambled to my feet, and I ran, without thinking, to the edge of the porch. I jumped off; I was going after her! I was going after her, and then, then my burning ears seized me so strong I tumbled to my knees. My eyes held fast to the woods, though, searching for the dog.

But there were only snowflakes. Silent snowflakes.

I limped back inside the cabin and sat down before the stove and pulled my trouser leg up over my right knee. It was skinned and bloodied from hitting the sharp-crusted snow. I felt the same way on the inside.

From the small bookstand next to Daddy's cot I fetched my history book and tried to settle into how Roman Emperor Constantine had been responsible for spreading the Christian faith all about the ancient world, but the questions racing through my mind and

EXTRAS

the longing that gripped me kept me on my feet, gimping back and forth across the cabin and pushing wide the door time after time.

"Do-og. Come! Come, dog," I shouted out through the snowy air again and again. But my voice sounded even smaller than before.